ANARCHY

Book 4 of
The Stone Legacy Series

Theresa DaLayne

Limitless Publishing, LLC
Kailua, HI 96734
www.limitlesspublishing.com

Formatting: Limitless Publishing

ISBN-13: 978-1-68058-515-5
ISBN-10: 1-68058-515-0

CHAPTER ONE

The glittering lights of the aurora wrapped around Zanya's body, spinning in a cyclone of ghostly blue, emerald green, and purple. The light in her chest, signifying her power as the Stone Guardian, beamed with life.

Jayden stepped back into the darkness, nearly tripping over his own feet, unable to tear his gaze from Zanya. The lights bonded souls, both in this world and in the afterlife. If they were touching Zanya, it could only mean one thing.

She was bonding with someone, and that someone wasn't him.

The crowds near the base of the temples gathered around their sacred fires with offerings of jade and maize. They cheered and chanted, beating on drums and dancing like the aboriginal Mayans once had, carrying out the tradition for thousands of years.

Jayden backed away from Zanya, nearly stumbling on protruding rocks half-buried in the grassy hill. Everyone in their group waited with wide eyes, their chests puffed out as if they held their breath, waiting for her soul mate to be revealed.

Jayden's gut tightened as the woman he would die for—*had* died for—reached for Arwan's hand.

It should have been *him* holding her close.

It should have been *him* kissing her.

He swallowed against a dry throat. It didn't make any sense. Arwan was half underworlder. Bonding with Riyata was forbidden. Hell, it was impossible. The two bloodlines simply weren't compatible.

Zanya's mother, Eleuia, trembled with fury. "I mean it," she demanded, her sharp gaze trained on Zanya. "Choose him," she jabbed her finger at Arwan, "or us. Because I won't allow that *thing* back in my house."

"For the gods' sake, Ellie," Renato pleaded.

"No!" She spun and glared at her brother. "You've done enough damage as it is. She is *my* daughter."

Jayden watched Zanya. She was so damn beautiful in that dress. He clenched his fists.

"You can't be serious," Zanya said, shaking her head. "How can you ask me to do that?" Her chest rose and fell with every quickened breath, her fingers now interlocked with Arwan's.

She held him so close, as if letting him go would ruin her. For the first time, Jay believed it actually would. She was bonded. Any chance he'd had with Zanya was lost.

A collection of cheers shook the air. Jayden looked at the crowd in the valley below. He'd almost forgotten where he was. With the lights retreating into the sky, the winter solstice celebrations had begun. Newly bonded couples were hugged and congratulated, though the Riyata group was far out of the crowd's reach.

"How can you guys just stand there and let her do this?" Zanya's desperate tone brought his focus back to her. It took a moment to realize she was speaking directly to him.

He parted his lips, but couldn't speak. He couldn't…wouldn't stand up for them. Not while everything he wanted was torn away. Not when he still loved her.

Zanya's gaze shifted to her best friend, Tara, who walked toward the newly bonded pair. "Yeah, this is messed up." Tara reached Zanya's side and faced the rest of the group, then crossed her arms over her chest. "They don't have any control over this stuff." She stared pointedly at the lights in the sky. "There's got to be something more going on here. Something you guys missed."

"Missed?" Eleuia's tone turned deadly. She stepped toward Zanya, who shifted in front of Arwan as if she were protecting him. "I didn't spend all this time hiding and running, to return to a piece of underworld garbage like him," she spat, glaring at Arwan. "He'll ruin our kind's only hope at a future. He is the reason I missed you growing up, Zanya. Why your father isn't here anymore."

Zanya flinched and dropped her head. Waves of her hair drifted in the warm breeze. "No, Mom." She lifted her chin, revealing a soft sheen in her eyes. "My father died because you fell in love with someone you weren't supposed to." She turned to face Arwan and took both of his hands.

Jayden's throat tightened and each breath grew harder to take as dread bore deep into his gut. He raked his fingers through his hair. *Shit*. He had to get the hell away. With Zanya bonded and her mom ready to light a torch and wave a pitchfork, things were about to get ugly. He'd be forced to choose. They all would. It was an impossible ultimatum.

If he chose Eleuia's side, it would mean turning his back on Zanya forever, because it would mean rejecting her bond with Arwan, and therefore, rejecting everything she was from this moment on.

But if he chose to stand by her, it would mean turning his back on his own heart.

Jayden looked away, at the sky, the ground, anywhere but at Zanya. He caught a glimpse of Hawa studying him. She held his gaze for a split second before he looked away.

He couldn't stay if he had to watch Zanya be with someone else, and he'd be damned if he spent another second as the pathetic ex-boyfriend who couldn't win her back.

Jayden analyzed his surroundings. The ruins of Tikal were crowded with parked cars for the celebration. Even the taxi drivers had abandoned their cabs to participate in the solstice.

He slipped away from the group and peered in car windows, one vehicle at a time. If he left on foot, traveling to…anywhere-but-here, would take twice as long. He needed a ride.

He paused when he spotted a pair of keys dangling from the ignition of a taxi. *Bingo*. He slipped into the driver's seat and turned the key. The engine roared to life. He took a moment to draw in a deep breath. Leaving was the only answer. Maybe now that his heart no longer beat, he was incapable of a real bond. He had to look out for himself. No one else would. He clutched the steering wheel tighter.

When he glanced in the rearview mirror, he was able to see the others, still crowded in a tight group, none of them realizing he was gone. Zanya backed away from her mother, drawing even closer to Arwan.

He ground his teeth. To hell with this.

Just as he shifted the car into drive, the passenger door flew open and Hawa launched herself inside, then slammed the door behind her. "Where do you think you're off to?"

He exhaled sharply. "Get out."

"Uh, not happening. I saw how you looked back there. There's no way I'm letting you take off alone."

He scoffed. "What do you care?"

"Who said I do?"

"Then get out." He leaned over her and pushed the door open.

Hawa bit her lip for a second while she watched him. "Look." She shut the door a second time. "I know how bad it sucks to watch the person you care about be with someone else."

Jayden relaxed his grip on the steering wheel. He'd almost forgotten that she and Peter used to be together, and she'd been forced to watch while the healer fell for Tara.

Hawa shrugged. "Plus, it'll be nice to get the hell out of the jungle for a while." She gestured to the path of crushed grass that passed for a makeshift road. "Well? Are we going or what?"

He hesitated, glanced once more in the rearview mirror, and then slammed his foot on the gas pedal. The rear end fishtailed before the tires bit into the ground.

He didn't look back.

A blur of green streaked by as he sped out of the jungle. Anger bubbled inside of him, paired with a deep humiliation. How could he have been so stupid? He never would have gotten Zanya back. It was just his luck. Always the underdog. Always the loser.

The tension in his muscles wound tighter until he couldn't stand it anymore. He balled his fist and punched the center of the steering wheel as hard as he could, honking the horn several times in the process. "That *wasn't* supposed to fucking happen!"

The car swerved and Hawa grabbed the wheel, preventing them from flying into the trees. "Whoa! Either pull over or calm the hell down before you get both of us killed!"

Jayden punched the steering wheel one more time, and then relieved some pressure from the gas. The car slowed to a reasonable speed.

"You good?" Hawa cautiously let go of the wheel.

He nodded, taking back control of the car. Both of them were silent the rest of the drive out of the jungle. He needed the time to think, and thankfully, Hawa wasn't one of those girls who couldn't shut up if her life depended on it.

He slowed when they reached a paved road,

making the ride smoother and a little easier to keep his shit together. At the moment, everything about the jungle pissed him off.

"You *do* realize when we get in town, the cops will probably be looking for this taxi, right?" Hawa slouched in the passenger seat and kicked one of her heavy leather boots up onto the dashboard, bobbing her foot left to right. "Unless the owner of the cab is too wasted to realize it's been taken until tomorrow morning. That would buy us a couple of hours."

That was the best-case scenario. It would give him enough time to figure out what he was going to do next, because now, all he knew for sure was he wouldn't go back to Renato's house. If Zanya was still there, she'd be there with Arwan. And if she wasn't, there was no reason to stick around anymore. It was a lose-lose scenario—the story of his entire fucking life.

"So, where to, *el capitán*?"

The muscles in his shoulders tensed at Hawa's voice. "I don't really know."

"Sweet." She flipped on the FM radio and fiddled with the stations until Latin music thumped from the speakers. She leaned back again, mouthing the lyrics.

He glanced at her. "That's it? You don't care that I have no idea where the hell we're going?"

She shrugged. "Not really. I'm always in for a good adventure."

"I'm *not* going back to Renato's house."

She yawned. "Let's roll down the windows." She leaned forward and used the hand crank to let the night air pour into the cab, then sat back, relaxing into her seat.

Since when did she want to be around him? She'd always just been the sprinter—able to travel at unimaginable speeds. She never cared about him. In fact, she gave off a *screw you* vibe every second of the day. Suddenly she was up for a road trip? Maybe she'd decide to split when they arrived at the next town…or maybe not. He glanced at her again, slouching with her eyes closed and black hair whipping wildly around her.

He swallowed as his stomach twisted and bubbled. Why was he so freaked out about her being around?

Jayden blinked and shook his head in an attempt to clear his mind.

He had to keep his shit together. He stole a quick look at the gas gauge. Full tank. Good. He'd drive through the night until they reached civilization. At least he didn't have to worry about getting tired anymore. He settled back in the seat. This whole kinda-dead thing had its advantages.

CHAPTER TWO

Sunrise crept over the distant horizon and cast bright light over Guatemala City. It had been so long since Jayden had witnessed a sunrise. Still, it didn't make up for the fact he'd spent all damn night driving, his thoughts trapped in a continuous loop of Zanya and Arwan's unexpected bonding. And now, after running away—something he'd sworn he'd never do—he had nowhere to go. Nowhere he belonged.

After he was forced to leave Zanya at the orphanage, the only hope that had kept him going was that he would one day be reunited with her. It took way longer than he'd expected, and by the time he found his way to Renato's, Zanya had not only come to terms with the fact he'd been gone for so long, she'd moved on. It'd been almost nine months since then. He'd learned a lot in that time. Mostly what an idiot he was for leaving her in the first place, no matter what Renato said.

For the last six hours of open road and silence, he'd searched his memories for a single instance

Zanya might have said she could love him again. Just one, fleeting instance when she'd led him to believe he had a chance, and they could somehow heal their broken relationship.

There was none.

Jayden tightened his grip on the steering wheel, his stomach in a solid knot. He was such a loser.

Hawa stretched her legs as much as she could in the passenger seat, and blinked open her sleep-glazed eyes. She yawned and smacked her lips, then groaned. "Coffee."

It was still so weird, having her around. "The city is just ahead." He scanned the glittering skyscrapers in the distance.

Hawa wiggled to sit upright. "Were you driving all night?" She pulled her raven hair back in a short ponytail.

"The city is only like a hundred and eighty miles from Tikal. I followed the signs."

"Nice." She drew in a deep breath. "Let's stop for something to eat when we get in town." She licked her lips. "I'm starving."

Jayden's mouth watered. He still had no idea why he became so hungry when he didn't sleep, especially since his heart wasn't beating anymore. Either way, he couldn't ignore the cramps in his stomach. "Sounds good to me."

He slowed at the first stoplight he'd seen in hours. The urban area housed huge steel buildings covered in thousands of windows, all reflecting the cityscape and sunlight. The streets were paved, two lanes wide, with crosswalks and people hustling to work or school. So different from Moscow or the rainforest of Belize, but a welcomed change.

He glanced at a blue and white sign bolted to a large brick building. "Yes, IHOP!" Jayden pulled in and parked near the entrance, then shut off the car. He tossed the keys to Hawa.

She dangled them from her finger. "What do you want me to do with these?"

He raised his eyebrows. "Don't you have a purse or something you can put them in?"

She rolled her eyes and threw the keys at him. They smacked into his chest and fell into his lap. Hawa scoffed. "Purses are for—"

"Girls?" He shoved the keys in his front pocket, where they'd dig into his hip and annoy the hell out of him. "Sorry for the mistake." He stepped out of the taxi he'd lifted from the solstice ceremony and slammed the door.

Hawa followed him out and shut the door, glaring over the hood. "I was going to say they're for people who didn't leave all their stuff behind, all to help out a guy who doesn't really deserve it."

"Like I said when you forced your way into the cab," he leaned against the hood of the car, "I didn't ask you to come."

She scoffed. "In case you've already forgotten, when you decided it was prime time to take off, Zanya's mom was pissed, and Zanya looked scared as hell. But you…" Her sharp gaze softened. "You seemed as scared as she did." She looked away and took a step back. "I left everyone behind too. Don't you forget it."

He exhaled and tore his gaze away from hers. "Right." He clenched his jaw. "Sorry."

"Yeah. Well, because of your stupid comment, *you're* buying breakfast." She strutted away, through the restaurant doors, leaving him to stand alone by the car.

He leaned on the metal hood, still warm from the long drive. He tilted his head, watching Hawa through the restaurant window. He could never really figure her out. The fact she matched him in sarcasm made their conversations unpredictable. He was the sarcastic one. That was how it had been with Zanya.

Jayden's throat tightened. For whatever reason, right now Hawa gave a shit what happened to him, and that was more than he could say for anyone else.

Now he just had to learn how not to be a total ass.

He walked into the restaurant, meeting a cute brunette with a beaming smile standing behind a podium. "Good morning. Just one?"

"Uh…" He scanned the restaurant for Hawa. "I actually came with someone. Black hair about to here." He pressed his fingers just below his shoulder. "Kinda bitchy."

The brunette's lips parted. She turned slightly and stared at Hawa, half-hidden in the corner at an awkwardly placed two-top. "Yep. That's her. Thanks." He walked to the table and sat.

Hawa leaned back in her chair, tapping her polished, purple fingernails on the table. "I seriously need a cup of coffee." Her gaze followed every waiter who passed. Her eyes narrowed when the third waiter walked by without stopping to take their order.

"Okay," Jayden said. "Just…chill out." He made eye contact with a waiter and flagged him over.

"Hey, sorry about that." The middle-aged man wearing a bluish apron took out a pad and pen. "What can I get ya for?"

"Two coffees," he said, holding up two fingers. "And a stack of blueberry pancakes, three eggs—over medium—a big glass of orange juice, two orders of turkey sausage, and some biscuits…with apple butter."

The waiter jotted the order down and then closed his notepad. "Be right—"

"Wait." He looked at Hawa. "Don't you want anything besides coffee?"

She arched a perfectly shaped eyebrow. "Hungry, are we?" She skimmed over her menu. "Low fat yogurt with granola and a fruit bowl." She extended her menu to the waiter.

"Got it." He took her menu and walked into the kitchen.

"You don't eat much, do you?" Jayden stretched his legs under the table and propped his feet on the chair beside Hawa.

She glanced at his sneakers and scrunched her nose. "Just because I'm not scarfing five-thousand calories doesn't mean I don't eat."

He had almost forgotten some girls actually thought about the whole calorie thing. Zanya had never—

He exhaled and slouched in his chair. It wouldn't do him any good to keep thinking about her. Not right now anyway. He needed some space. Some time to figure out how the hell he was going to still be her friend while being forced to watch her and Arwan live happily ever after like Cinderella and Prince-Fucking-Charming.

Hawa cleared her throat, snapping him out of his thoughts. "So." She unfolded her napkin and laid it in her lap. "What are we doing after this?" He analyzed her movements—so careless and easy. Strands of hair had fallen out of her ponytail and were scattered on either side of her angled cheekbones. She didn't seem even a little concerned that she'd taken off with him in a stolen cab, or that everyone would be worried about her. And they *would* be worried. She may be snarky, short-tempered, and the way she rolled her eyes at him plucked every nerve in his body, but she was Renato's niece. Unlike Jayden, she was part of the family, and they would want her back, sooner or later.

She picked up the dessert menu and scanned through the pages.

Jayden watched her read through a list of chocolate cakes and raspberry toppings, like she would actually eat any of it. "What's your deal?"

Her head bobbed up as if his question caught her off guard. "What do you mean?"

"Why come with me? I hardly know you, and your uncle and the rest of his groupies are probably wondering where you are."

She shrugged. "I needed to get away, and I saw an opportunity."

He peered at her. "That's it?"

"Yeah. That's it. So don't go reading into it,

okay?" She pushed away the menu and sat back, mumbling in Spanish.

The waiter returned with two steaming cups of coffee. "The food should be up in about ten minutes."

Jayden nodded, and the waiter vanished back into the kitchen.

"Thank God." Hawa poured some cream into her cup. She cradled the coffee with both hands and inhaled the aroma before lifting it to her lips. Her shoulders visibly relaxed.

Good. Now maybe she wouldn't rip his throat out.

As he reached for the creamer, a deep tremor ran up his arm, over his shoulder, and crawled up his neck, exploding in a flash of light, stripping him of his vision.

He closed his eyes and ground his teeth. An image of Contessa appeared. The evil witch cradled a book under one arm. She looked like shit, but her powers were still strong. Her darkness radiated onto him, inducing a spout of nausea.

"Hey." Hawa's harsh whisper yanked him out of the vision. His eyes flew open. She leaned on the table toward him and glanced around the restaurant. "What the hell was that?"

"I don't know." His seeking ability hadn't worked since his soul returned from the underworld. Unlike when he was still in control of his ability, this vision materialized without his consent. He rubbed his eyes. Bizarre. He didn't want to find her. He hadn't closed his eyes and focused on her face, voice, or a vivid memory. It just…happened. "I think…" He dropped his hands into his lap and blinked, clearing the fuzzy border from the edges of his vision. "I think I just sought Contessa…somehow." He rubbed his eyes again. If his ability were to come back, maybe that meant other things would come back too—like his pulse.

"Well," she sat back and crossed her arms over her chest, "if you start to feel the urge to bite a chunk out of my arm, make sure to tell me so I can get as far away from you as possible."

"What?" He ran his fingers through his hair and down his face, willing away the headache throbbing through his temples.

"You *were* in the underworld. If weirder-than-normal seeking stuff is happening, who says you won't turn all zombie apocalypse sometime when you're hungry?"

He couldn't help but chuckle at her tight features and puckered lips. The sprinter was dead serious. "I'm not a zombie." Great. The only semi-normal conversation he'd ever had with her, and it had her worrying he'd chew her face off.

He picked up his cup of coffee and sipped it, deciding it best to drink it black. The waiter returned with a tray of food, and another waiter behind him.

Jayden's stomach rumbled at the scent of the turkey sausage and buttery biscuits. For a second he'd forgotten how hungry he was. After a good meal, they would figure out what to do next. But since he hadn't thought to bring cash to the solstice with him, he was totally broke. Too bad he hadn't remembered that little fact before ordering. He'd have to tell Hawa they were going to dine and dash.

If he weren't already dead, he'd be afraid she'd kill him.

Chapter Three

"I can't believe you don't have any cash," Hawa whispered harshly over the table, full of empty plates. "How were you planning to pay for the mountains of food you just got through inhaling?"

Jayden scratched the nervous itch pinching at the back of his arm. "I didn't exactly plan on *any* of this."

She scoffed and rested the heel of her boot on the edge of her chair, her thigh pressed to her chest, and dug in the top of her boot.

"What are you going to do?" he mumbled while she tugged and pulled at the zipper. "Hope they love your fashion sense and let us walk?"

She retrieved a wad of cash and rested her foot back on the floor. "I'm going to pay for our food, jackass."

He sat up straight, watching her count out five and ten dollar bills onto the table. "You said you didn't have any money."

She laid down the last five-dollar bill and shoved the rest into her bra. "I said I left my stuff behind. I always have a little cash, just in case." She stood. "And I don't believe in stealing."

Jayden pushed out of his chair and followed her through the crowded restaurant, out to the parking lot. When she slowed, he continued toward the cab.

"Nope."

He paused. "What do you mean, 'nope'?"

"Leave it. It's too risky." She gestured toward the street. "We'll get around on foot."

He shoved his hand in his pocket and pulled out the keys. Maybe if he left them with the car, the driver wouldn't be quite as pissed. "Okay. Hang on a second." Jayden opened the driver's side door, tucked the keys in the sun visor, and then used his shirt to wipe the steering wheel and doors clean of any fingerprints.

"Ready?" Hawa tapped her foot on the pavement.

"If you helped, this would go faster," he mumbled before locking the door and slamming it shut. "I don't want to attract any unwanted attention with fingerprints."

"Says the walking dead guy." Hawa strutted down the sidewalk and vanished around the corner.

Jayden exhaled. She was *such* a pain in the ass. He followed her around the corner of a brick building. She stood on the sidewalk beside a four-lane street, waiting for the signal on the crosswalk to change. Apparently, she knew her way around. Good thing, because he had no clue. He jogged to catch up. She jabbed the crosswalk button again, as if that would make the light change any faster.

"I know a hotel we can stay at."

"Oh, good." Especially since she'd said *we,* which meant he wasn't sentenced to a night out in the cold. Jayden peered up at the morning sun. "But it's kinda early to check in, isn't it?"

"If we don't secure a spot to crash, we may both end up staying in an alley. Plus, we can't afford anything fancy, so the place I have in mind will have to do." The signal changed and she walked toward the other side of the street.

He followed closely, observing her confident stride. "I guess you know your way around here pretty well."

They reached the other side of the street right as the signal changed back to a blinking red hand. She pointed down the road, where even higher buildings towered in the distance. Cars zoomed down the busy street, spewing the bitter scent of exhaust into the air. "I used to stay with some friends downtown, before I moved in with Renato."

He stared deep into downtown. "Oh. So you lived here?"

She glanced at him and then took off walking again, her clunky leather boots pounding against the ground with every step. "Kinda. I went to Renato like a year ago. Before that I just visited, mostly after my parents..." She blinked and cleared her throat. "After my parents died in this shitty war our kind has been fighting for the last umpteen million years." She picked her pace up again. "He asked me to stay so many times, but I didn't really trust him." She tucked her hair behind her ear. A thick silver ring glinted from around her middle finger. "But when you're sixteen and don't have a ton of options, a huge mansion and an uncle willing to let me stay as long as I wanted seemed pretty damn good." She exhaled. "It was cool while it lasted, but I missed the place I grew up. I missed the kids, mostly. They're what really made it feel like home."

Kids? Home? Who is *this chick?*

"So you were…" He paused, but didn't really know how else to say it. "You were a wanderer or something?" Ditched by your parents was more accurate, but he was really working on the whole *not being such an asshole* thing.

"Not by their own choice." She analyzed his reaction—or lack there off—and then rolled her eyes. "Never mind. You wouldn't understand." Her stride quickened and she pushed ahead.

"What makes you think I wouldn't understand?" He jogged a few steps to catch up to her and fell into pace.

"Forget it."

He waited for her to cave, but she never did. Women were so damn confusing. They said one thing and meant another, or said something with the expectation he'd say something back, but every time he did, it just pissed them off even more. He slouched his shoulders.

It seemed like they'd been walking forever before Hawa paused to examine the streets. She silently made a left, and then another quick right into a narrow side street that was dark and smelled like piss. Jayden pushed down the urge to gag. "Where are you going?"

"To the hotel."

He peered up between two huge buildings.

Graffiti tagged the crumbling walls below clotheslines strung over rusted balconies, hinting they were in the projects. "The hotel is *here*? Seems like it'll be a rat hole."

"It'll have what we need. A bed. A shower."

"A TV?" Jayden waited in anticipation.

Hawa shook her head. "No TV."

He frowned, but couldn't complain, considering she was flipping the bill for them both. She stopped beside an old door with peeling orange paint. A burnt-out neon sign he almost didn't notice hung over the entrance. "This is it?"

"Just shut up and follow my lead." Hawa knocked with three solid pounds of her fist. She waited a second, and then pounded three more times.

It seemed she knew what she was doing, though it didn't make much sense to him. "Don't people just walk into the lobby of hotels?"

"Shh."

The door creaked open. A kid who didn't look over the age of ten stood on the other side. His eyes lit up. "Holy shit!" He turned and shouted into the hotel. "Hey, guys! It's Brisa. She's back!"

Hawa reached out and ruffled the boy's messy, auburn hair. "Hey, watch your language, punk."

"*Brisa*?" Jayden asked.

"It's what they called me here," she said quietly. "It means breeze in Spanish."

"I can't believe you're back!" The kid shuffled aside and swung open the door.

A guy with brown hair and a knife strapped to his belt stepped behind the boy. He smirked and rested his hand on the blade's handle. "So, you've fallen off your silk pillow, huh, *mamacita*?"

Hawa pursed her lips and avoided eye contact, looking toward the ground. "Hey, Rico."

"People around these parts still call me Blade, if you don't remember."

She shrugged, still not making eye contact, and gave a nod. "Sure." She gestured to Jayden. "We need somewhere to squat for a while."

Jayden leaned in close to her. "I thought we were going to a hotel," he whispered. Hawa elbowed him in the ribs. He grunted, and then took a step back. Time to shut up.

Blade examined Jay with a deep stare. His eyes narrowed. "The *gringo* can't come in. Only *familia*."

Hawa finally raised her gaze. "But we're together. Can't you make an exception? You're the *vato* calling the shots."

Blade tilted his head. "Are you and the *gringo* together?"

Hawa glanced at Jayden, then scoffed. "Not like that. Just traveling together. So can we squat, or not?"

The young boy inched toward Blade and tugged on his shirt. "You have to let her in, Blade. She's *familia*. The code says we can't turn her away."

The code? What the hell kind of underground secret society did Hawa drag him into? Whatever it was, he wasn't going to stick around to find out.

Jayden slowly backed away. "Hey, listen. Clearly this is some kind of...I don't know, personal thing you guys got going on. I'll just take off. No big deal." He glanced at the sprinter, whose glare deepened as he spoke.

"No." Blade rested his hand on the door, pushing it open further. "Tic-Tac's right. It's code. Any friend of Brisa's is a friend of ours." He stepped aside and gestured for them to enter. "Welcome to the Thirteenth Street Hotel, *camaradas*."

CHAPTER FOUR

Jayden followed Hawa inside the hotel. The guy to his left—Blade, as he called himself—smirked, his attention trained on Hawa.

Something about that guy put Jay on edge. Maybe it was the cocky air about him, or maybe it was because he had a tattoo of a fucking snake wrapped around his twenty-inch bicep.

But not just a snake. A python.

What a douche.

At least Jayden's tattoos were artistic. Blade's insinuated he was overcompensating for something.

Blade shut the door to the hotel, overrun with guests. "I have to go take care of a few things." He walked toward them, pausing beside Jayden. "You two just make yourselves at home." He patted Jay on the shoulder and winked. In guy language, it pretty much translated to, *"Don't make any trouble, and if you touch Hawa, I'll tear your balls off."*

Jayden clenched his jaw. Blade's hand slipped off his shoulder and he walked away. "What was that all about?" Jayden said in a low voice.

"Don't worry about him. He just likes to remind people he's in charge."

"Right." Jayden pumped his fists. He got the message loud and clear. Too bad he gave exactly zero fucks.

"Come on." Hawa waved him forward. "Follow me."

Jayden did exactly what she asked. This was no regular hotel. The entire population in sight ranged in age from around six to eighteen, if he had to guess. But most were kids. Young kids, around middle school age.

Every door to every hotel room hung open. A young girl sat on top of the check-in counter, swinging her feet side to side. The tan, weathered paint flaked off as the soles of her worn sneakers rubbed against it.

A group of younger children played around the empty stone fountain in the center of the lobby. Had that thing ever had water? Maybe a long time ago, though now it was filled with empty plastic bottles and random scraps of trash. Surprisingly, it didn't stink.

The echo of shouts made him crank his neck upward. He spotted a few kids inching along the outside of the railing on their tiptoes, two stories up. "What is this place, exactly?"

"Like he said," Hawa replied. "The Thirteenth Street Hotel." She spent a long moment scanning their surroundings. "This place looks like shit," she mumbled. "What the hell happened?"

"Brisa!" A girl, who couldn't have been older than twelve, ran toward them. Her frizzy ponytail bobbed with every step until she threw her arms around Hawa's waist. "Blade told all of us you weren't coming back. What changed your mind?"

He caught the glimpse of a frown turn down the corners of her lips, but Hawa quickly gave the girl a smile. "I missed you guys. That's what changed my mind." She hugged the girl against her hip. "You couldn't have done all this growing in two years."

The girl giggled. When she noticed Jayden, her smile vanished. "Is he your boyfriend?"

Hawa's eyebrows rose. "Not even close. This is Jayden. Jay, this is Chastity. We call her Modem, on account of she can hack into just about anything."

"That's right." Modem's brown eyes were warm and bright. "I'm the best hacker between here and Fifty-Fourth Street."

"And she's a little thief too. So watch your stuff." Hawa tugged on the girl's ponytail.

Modem raised her hand. "Excuse me. I don't steal. I borrow. There's a difference."

"Mhm." Hawa pointed two fingers to her eyes, then at Modem. "I'll have my eyes on you." She looked at Jay. "Come on. Let's get a room before they're all gone."

Jayden followed Hawa deeper into the hotel. She rested her hand on the steel railing to the stairs and looked up at rows of endless doors and staircases, and people walking freely through the halls. "I used to stay in room 409. Let's go see if it's vacant…or standing." She rubbed her fingers together and crinkled her nose.

Fantastic. She'd brought him to a dirty, rundown

orphanage, run by a guy who called himself *Blade*. The next time she said they were going to a hotel, he'd ask for more details. He snorted, and then gestured to the elevator. "Does this at least work?"

She shook her head. "Hasn't since I can remember."

"Of course." He followed behind her as they scaled the stairs.

"What electricity we do have is jacked from some spliced lines. We don't really worry about overusing it since the lines lead to the downtown corporate buildings." She shrugged. "They never noticed."

"I thought you didn't believe in stealing."

"Well, if someone took care of these kids, we wouldn't be forced to." They reached the top of the stairs and continued down the hall toward a dead end.

His throat closed as a searing pain shot through his temples. He fell to his knees and grabbed onto the metal bars lining the catwalk.

An image of Contessa tore through his mind. Her eyes glowed bright with magic as she read from the book. The atmosphere rippled, and Contessa's head shot up. She stared directly at him, as if she could see him. As if she knew he was seeking her. Her eyes narrowed, and she stood upright, her stare focused in his direction, her gaze flickering from side to side, searching. For him?

"Get up!" Hawa's voice shattered the vision, and Jay opened his eyes to everyone in the hotel standing silent, watching him. Hawa hooked her arm under his and hauled him off the ground. He leaned on her, struggling to peer through his blurred vision. "You have got to stop doing that," she ordered. "Come on. Let's get you into a room."

Though he didn't necessarily *need* to sleep anymore, now that he had no heartbeat, he could, and was grateful to have a place to lie down and rest. Hawa pushed open the door and helped him inside. The room was empty except a rollout mattress laid out on the worn, patterned carpet. Good enough for him. He lay down and pressed his hands over his eyes. "Damn it, that hurt."

"Did you see Contessa again?"

"Yeah, but I don't understand why I'm seeing her. It's not like I'm doing it on purpose. I wasn't even thinking about her. It just happened."

"Has your ability always had a mind of its own?"

He shook his head. "Not until I died."

"Well, until we figure it out, you need to stay away from crowds. If Blade even thinks you're a threat to the kids, he'll kick your ass out, or worse."

"So I'll leave," Jayden grumbled. "Who gives a damn what Blade thinks?" He lifted his hands from his eyes and blinked up at her. "Who is he, anyway?"

Hawa walked to the window. "He's the one who watches over the kids." She glanced back at him. "And he's dangerous. Don't screw with him, Jay. I'm serious."

He grunted while forcing himself to sit up, and rested his back against the wall. "Why did you bring us here?"

"Because we needed a place to stay, and neither of us has the money to stay in a real hotel for more than a few nights, and then we wouldn't have cash for food."

He paused. "Okay, good point." He rested his head against the wall. A few sharp slams on the door made him flinch.

Hawa turned and faced the door. "What?"

"Open the door, Brisa." Jayden immediately recognized Blade's voice.

"Shit." Hawa glared at Jayden. "See what you did?" She opened the door to reveal Blade on the other side, his features like stone.

He pushed past her into the room and stared down at Jay, who tried his best not to look like a bag of smashed assholes. "What's wrong with you?" Blade demanded.

Jayden pushed to his feet, fighting off the cyclone in his head. "Nothing. I'm fine." He flattened his palm against the wall to stabilize himself.

Blade glanced back at Hawa. "You know what the rule is about bringing a risk into the hotel."

"I know," Hawa said. "But he's not—"

Blade squared his shoulders and faced her. "Don't you think for a second you get a pass on the rules. Our history doesn't affect a damn thing, and code or not, I'll throw you out on your ass before I let you bring some *chabón* in here if there's a reason he shouldn't be here. *¿Entiendes?*"

Hawa didn't look scared as much as on high alert. Her gaze flickered between him and Blade until she settled on the douche with the snake tattoo. She nodded.

Jayden stepped away from the wall. "Hey. Lay

off. She didn't break any of your precious codes." Whatever this guy's problem was, Jay didn't love how he talked to Hawa. Pain in the ass or not, she'd stuck by him when no one else did.

Blade fisted his hands. "Are you sick? Because if you are, it could spread, and the hospitals here don't give a damn about an orphan kid with no way to pay his hospital bill."

Even if he were sick, it wasn't the kind of sick that could spread…he hoped. "I'm just tired as hell. Haven't had a good night's rest in—" Well, since he died, but he would just skip over that part. "In a long time." He held Blade's gaze. "That's it."

Blade examined him a moment longer, then gave a single nod. "Good. Make sure it stays that way." He walked toward the door and paused beside Hawa. "I mean it." His tone had calmed, and the focus in his stare unsettled Jay. "I know you've been gone for a while, but don't let that silver spoon in your mouth distort your idea of what role you play here. It's not like it used to be."

Hawa swallowed and then nodded.

Blade held eye contact with her for a moment longer, then walked out of the room. Hawa's chest fell in a deep exhale. She clutched her stomach.

When she didn't say anything, Jayden stepped toward her. "Hey. You okay?"

Hawa dropped her hand to her side and nodded. "Yeah. I'm fine." The words came out in a near whisper. She cleared her throat and then walked toward the hall. "You should get some rest. I'm going to visit a few of the kids and see if they need anything. This place has really gone to hell since I left, and I want to check it out a little closer. Then we have some work to do in the hotel to earn our keep."

"But—"

She stopped and spun to face him. "But nothing, Jay. Everyone earns their keep around here. No exceptions. If you don't, you're out."

Jayden nodded, and she left the room.

He wasn't entirely comfortable with the idea of staying in the hotel, or anywhere near that Blade guy. But if he were honest with himself, he had nothing better to do, and these people clearly meant something to Hawa. So he'd stick around. For now.

CHAPTER FIVE

That night while Hawa slept, Jay paced the length of the hotel room wall, the silent, still darkness outside his window reminding him that he had nowhere to go and no plans for his future.

He needed to figure out a way to get his seeking ability under control, and fast. But that would require practice.

Maybe he would try to seek Hawa. At least if he sought *her*, he wouldn't accidentally see something that would make him want to gouge his eyes out—like Zanya and jungle-boy shacked up together. The idea made his stomach turn.

Jayden closed his eyes and concentrated on Hawa's sleek hair and rich, olive skin. He tried to remember the smooth texture of her voice. How her hips swayed when she walked. How every time she looked at him, her eyes were like a deep, dark cave holding a world of secrets she'd never let him reach. He tuned in to anything that would guide his mind to where she slept, just a few feet away.

Static shook behind his eyelids, and his effort

slammed into a steel barrier in his mind. He fisted his hands and leaned against the wall. If he could push through the block, just once, it could free him from the mental prison he was living in. He bore down and rammed harder against the haze. With each attempt, his mind took another blow, and what little energy he had left quickly dissolved.

Jayden exhaled and pressed his forehead against the cool, textured wallpaper, both of his palms pressed on either side of his head.

"What are you doing?" Hawa's said in a groggy voice.

Jayden blinked and looked at her. She lay with her cheek cradled against a thin wool blanket. "Nothing," he said softly. "Go back to sleep." He hung his head. "Sorry if I woke you."

"Were you trying to seek her?"

He lifted his head. "Who?"

Hawa's honey brown eyes shimmered in the silky moonlight pouring through the crack in the curtains. "Zanya."

He paused and shoved his hands in his pockets. "No. I was, uh…" He glanced up at her. "I was trying to seek you, actually."

"Me?" Her brow furrowed. "But I'm right here."

"I know. I thought if I could just…" He leaned against the closed door. "Never mind." There was no point in explaining it to her. She'd never understand.

Hawa blinked and sat up. "What?"

He swallowed. "I just wanted to see if I could do it. That's all." A long moment of silence lingered between them.

She turned her face the window. White moonlight washed over her features. "I have a question."

"Sure." He slid down the wall and crouched to be eye to eye with her.

Hawa twisted the thin blanket draped over her lap. "What made you so crazy about her? I mean, you love her even though she doesn't feel the same. How do you do that?"

"*How* do I love her?" He didn't quite understand the question, or why she'd asked it.

"I mean…" She stole a glance at him. "How can you stand to?"

"I…" He thought about it for a moment. It was a question he'd never asked himself, until now. "I guess the truth is I don't think about it. It's how I feel, and I've never been the kind of guy to run away." He shifted his weight. "Regardless of what everyone else may think."

Hawa shook her head. "I respect my uncle, but he and the rest of them are blind. They don't get it. They never have. They always want to be around people. They want to be close to family and rely on others. But the second you do, that person always finds a way to leave you alone. Not being attached is way easier. I know that now."

He took a moment to observe the sprinter. She sat with her legs crossed and sadness deepening the creases around her mouth. There was a sense of desperation in her eyes. She too wanted to get away from the constant reminder of never being able to find happiness. Maybe even more than he did.

"I guess it's just our luck," she said. "Falling for

people who don't love us back." She flashed a smile, even though it was a little sad. "I guess we're more alike than I thought." Hawa lay down and closed her eyes. "Good night, Jay."

He quietly lowered the rest of his body to the floor and kicked his legs out in front of him, watching as the sprinter's shoulders rose and fell with every breath.

She was right. It was his luck, but nobody changed their own luck by sitting on their ass. Tomorrow he'd figure out what he'd do now that he was free to go where he wanted without taking orders, or having to worry the girl he loved would be torn away from him. That ship had sailed.

He needed to move on.

Tomorrow.

He closed his eyes.

He'd figure it all out tomorrow.

With his back pressed against the wall, his muscles relaxed and he drifted off to sleep. As his mind floated between asleep and awake, he was pulled into a layer of his subconscious he had never explored.

Standing in a space cloaked in darkness, images wavered in front of him, shadowed and indiscernible. A familiar power lingered nearby. Jayden peered closer at the images. It was as if he stood outside some kind of barrier that rippled and moved like a wall of water. Its cool iridescence gave light to the endless space.

He reached out and skimmed his fingers along the wavering surface. The air around him seemed to shudder. He pulled his hand back to his chest. After scrutinizing the barrier for a moment, he hesitated, and then touched it again. The wall stretched away from his skin.

He examined his fingers carefully. No damage that he could see, but considering he couldn't feel pain anymore, there was no way to be sure. He reached toward the barrier again, and it stretched further, moving away from his body as he grew close. He stepped toward it, and the entire wavering wall continued forward, as if it were moving with him.

Heat from the sand scorched his skin. As he walked over solid, cracked soil, he noticed patches of brownish-red liquid dried nearly to dust under the hot sun. Sun that seemed so close, he could barely breathe.

Jay shielded his eyes and stared up at a sky of soil and roots writhing above him, somehow coexisting with the burning sun. "What the fuck..."

A familiar voice caught his attention, and he turned to see a watery image of Contessa sitting on the other side of the barrier, on the bottom steps of a Mayan temple, just yards away. He focused and her image sharpened. A stack of blood-smeared papers lay cradled in her lap. He walked toward her. The watery wall rolled in front of him until he stood mere feet away.

Contessa rocked back and forth, whispering as she read a passage aloud.

Jayden examined the witch, who didn't seem to notice he was there. Hell, he didn't know how he got there. But his ability had linked him with

Contessa several times already. There had to be a reason why.

Contessa hadn't glanced up from the pages, so he continued to creep toward her until he stood at her side. He examined the pages from what had to be the Popul Vuh, the book she'd stolen from Zanya's nemesis. He couldn't read any of the ancient symbols etched over the pages.

Contessa's red, wavy hair and milky skin glistened like a mirage. She was beautiful, there was no denying it. And she looked a thousand times better than she had the first time his ability linked them. Maybe she was getting stronger.

Jayden pivoted and scanned the horizon. There was nothing but desolation, and marks on the ground from what seemed to be some kind of battle.

When Jay turned back toward Contessa, she rested her head in her hands, sobbing like a heartbroken child. The earth under his feet trembled, bouncing tiny pebbles and grains of sand in every direction. A massive, roaring sound filled his ears.

He spun toward a sea of water as the barrier charged toward him like a tsunami. When the waves crashed into him, he gasped and opened his eyes to the dark room.

Hawa was still lying there, asleep on the mattress.

CHAPTER SIX

The next morning, Jayden woke to an empty hotel room. The door was propped open, and the blanket Hawa had slept under the night before was folded and placed at the foot of the mattress.

He picked himself off the floor and cautiously moved into the hall to scout for her. She had to be somewhere close—if she hadn't ditched him completely. He leaned against the cold metal railing and peered down at the crowds of kids loitering inside the hotel lobby. It was a weekday, and none of them were in school. They probably didn't go at all.

Hawa walked through the front entrance wearing a pair of dark wash jeans and a white T-shirt with a low neckline—different clothes than she'd worn the day before. Jayden wove down the flights of stairs until he reached the bottom floor. His shoes scuffed against the old wood, worn and abused from years of neglect.

Hawa flashed an awkward smile. "Hey. I'm glad you're awake." She tossed a shirt at him.

It smacked him in the chest and he fumbled not to let it drop to the floor. "What's this?" Jay held up a blue polo shirt and crinkled his nose. "Trying to say I'd look better dressed like a prep?"

Hawa grinned, eyeing him. "I didn't say that, but you never know. Maybe you should try to change your look every once in a while." She passed him with that confident trademark strut.

"Hey." Jay took a few quick steps to catch up with her. "Where did you get the clothes, anyway?"

"Thrift store." She flipped her hair over her shoulder. "You can wash what you're wearing in the sink and hang them next to the window in our room to dry, but we don't want you wandering around naked, meanwhile."

He felt the cotton fabric between his fingers. "So…you actually bought this for me?"

Hawa glanced over her shoulder at him. "Don't make a *thing* out of it. I just didn't want to smell you."

"Brisa!" The little girl they called Modem threw her arms around Hawa's waist. "Where have you been? I've been looking all over for you." She grabbed Hawa by the hand and dragged her forward.

Hawa glanced over her shoulder at Jayden as she was pulled away. "Come on." Hawa waved him forward. "We need to talk, and Modem won't leave me alone until she shows me what she has."

Jayden followed them into a hallway, to the last hotel room on the right. The inside was packed with stacks of disassembled electronics and flashing computer parts with spliced wires joined with others to make what he could only assume was some kind of semi-genius, semi-insane computer laboratory. Each outlet in the room had either an extension cord or a second outlet plug with five or six more plugs attached, everything jam-packed and full to capacity.

Modem let go of the sprinter's hand and rushed to a computer screen sitting on the floor. She stooped beside a keyboard and tapped on the keys, then hit enter. The girl shot up to her feet and extended her hands, doing jazz fingers. "Ta da!" Jayden glanced around the room, waiting for whatever she'd done to be obvious so he didn't feel like such an ass, but nothing happened. "Pretty cool, huh?" Modem leaned against the wall. She crossed her arms and tilted her head to the side with a proud smirk.

Jayden whispered to Hawa. "I don't get it."

Modem's brow furrowed. "Of course you don't get it." She rolled her eyes and let out a heavy sigh. "Only people who know about hacking into the cable network get it. And that's not you."

Hawa laughed, and he was almost sure it was the first time he'd ever seen her genuinely smile. She was actually kinda…pretty.

"Modem's a huge fan of all things top secret." Hawa held out her fist, and the girl bumped it with her own smaller fist.

"We just got free cable, thanks to my mad skills," Modem said. She hooked her thumbs in the front pockets of her jeans. "Like I said, I'm the best hacker between here and Fifty-Fourth Street."

"So, the big news is…" Jayden rubbed the back

of his neck. "You guys have TV now?"

"That's right." Hawa ruffled the kinky curls on the girl's head. "We have TV." She pointed at Modem, and the girl's smile vanished. "But only the educational stuff, all right? No staying up late to watch scary movies."

"What about—"

"*No.* No *Chainsaw Massacre.* I'm not even kidding."

Modem blew out a puff of air. "Fine. I got the cable more for the little kids, anyway." She walked past Jayden, holding his gaze. "Besides." She stopped beside him and scanned his body, as if she were sizing him up. "I have more interesting things to do at night these days."

Jayden shifted his weight. "What's that supposed to mean?"

Modem shrugged, and then walked out of the room, leaving him and Hawa alone once again.

"Man." Jayden shook his head. "That kid is something."

"She's a genius." Hawa sighed. "Too bad her parents couldn't raise her. She could have been the next Steve Jobs." Hawa tapped her index finger on her temple. "She's so damn smart, but she's too busy using her talents for stuff that'll only waste her life."

"She's just a kid. You can cut her some slack."

"Around here, being a kid stops when you're old enough to pick pockets or beg on the street. The *really* young ones get taken care of. But Modem..." Hawa stared at the empty doorway as if the girl were still there. "She grew up way too fast."

Jayden didn't respond. He wasn't sure how. Kids and the whole maternal instinct thing were way beyond him. He'd thought it way beyond Hawa too. But after she'd led him here, to this abandoned hotel all these kids called home, it was obvious her past was way more complicated than he'd thought, and her emotional well wasn't nearly as shallow.

"Anyway." Hawa gestured to the shirt in Jayden's hand. "Change and we'll get down to business."

"What business?"

"Uh, figuring out why your ability is freaking out and you're seeing Contessa every five seconds. Obviously."

"Oh. Right." Jayden turned, giving her his back. Not that he was shy to change in front of her, but his chest was still jacked up from Sarian's attack and it was taking way longer to heal than he'd thought. Even after Peter and Zanya had both worked to heal him, it had only gotten so much better.

Turned out dead guys didn't heal so well.

He slipped off his shirt and drew the new one over his head. Once he'd pulled it over his chest, he turned back to face her. "Done. Let's go."

"Go?"

Jayden shifted his weight. "Yeah. You said we had to 'get down to business.' You…" He quickly scanned the room. "You wanna do it here?"

Hawa snorted. "You make it sound like we're going to sneak off to have a quickie." She shut and locked the door to Modem's room. "Just chill out. We need to figure out how to access your ability without it making you double over."

"Good luck. I tried yesterday and it was an epic fail."

She turned and leaned against the door, analyzing him. "You haven't tried everything or you would have figured it out." She pushed off the door and walked toward him. "The good news is we know you still have your ability." She rested her hands on her hips and peered at him. "The bad news is you have no idea how to access it without it going rogue." She crossed one arm over her chest and tapped an index finger against her lips while thinking. Jayden's eyes flickered down to her cleavage.

Shit.

He immediately trained his gaze to the floor.

Don't look at the sprinter's boobs.

Don't look at the sprinter's boobs.

"Wow. You really need to work on your bedside manners." She tugged up on the neckline of her top.

Jayden froze and slowly dragged his gaze to her face. "What did you just say?"

"I said you don't have to be so obnoxious. You act like you've never seen cleavage before."

"You...you heard me?"

Hawa snorted. "Don't look at the sprinter's boobs," she mimicked in an obnoxious tone. "You got some drool..." she brushed her finger over the corner of her mouth, "right there."

Dread settled in his bones. "I didn't say that aloud." He slumped against the wall and rubbed his face. "Either that or I'm going bat shit crazy."

"I'd say that's the more probable option."

"I'm going to try something. Turn around." She hesitated, and then did what he asked.

"Okay." He brushed his fingers together. "Now just…listen." The room fell silent. Jayden shut his eyes and thought of the name of his favorite band.

"What's that?"

Jayden's eyes shot open. "What is *what*?" The last word came out in a soft, low tone.

Hawa turned to face him. "The Ataris. Atris…whatever. I don't know what that is."

Jayden exhaled a sharp breath and swallowed down the lump in his throat.

Hawa's lips pressed into a tight line. "You better tell me what's going on."

Jayden clenched and unclenched his jaw. He ran his hands over his hair and wove his fingers together behind his head.

"Hey…" Hawa's tone had softened. "What's going on?"

"I didn't say *The Ataris*."

"Okay? What did you say, then?"

"No. You don't get it. I didn't *say* it. I thought it. And you heard me."

CHAPTER SEVEN

"What the hell do you mean, you *thought* it?" Hawa narrowed her eyes.

"Exactly what I said. I didn't *say* anything."

"So…you're telepathic now?"

"How the hell should I know?" He pressed his eyes shut and ground his teeth. This was too much. One second he was alive, the next he wasn't, then he was stuck in the underworld sharing bunk space with a trillion other souls for way longer than he cared to remember, and then he was alive again—but not really—and now his ability had gone rogue. That, or totally changed. If there was a limit for weird, this had to be it.

A steady ticking prompted Jayden to open his eyes. Hawa stood, tapping her boot on the wood floor, biting the inside of her cheek. "It seems like your ability has morphed. Changed. But into what?" She stopped tapping her foot and cocked her head to the side. "How far away can I be? I mean…" She backed up a few steps. "Can you think something loud enough for me to hear it all the way across the room?"

Jayden shrugged and rubbed the back of his neck. Suddenly, he didn't want to explore this new power anymore. The way she looked at him made him feel like a freak, and the last thing he wanted to be, now that he'd gotten away from Renato's calculating stare, was a different kind of freak. Been there, done that. "I…" His jaw ticked. "I don't know. I don't want to do this right now." He stormed past her, flung open the door, and charged down the hall, turning sideways to squeeze between kids kicking around a half-inflated ball.

"Hey," Hawa called out in a harsh whisper. Jayden didn't look back. He quickened his pace until he reached the side door near the alley, and swung open the door.

Blade stood in the shadowed street below the dead neon sign, talking to some guy in a hoodie. Blade turned and stared at Jayden, then arched his eyebrows. "Going somewhere?"

Jayden pushed past them. "I'm leaving. Thanks for the *hospitality*."

"Stop." The word was a command rather than a suggestion, and Jayden wasn't in the mood. He had to get out of there before he did something he'd regret—something that reflected the mounting weight in his gut and the sweltering heat that accompanied it. Talking to Blade wouldn't help cure that. Besides, Hawa could have caught up with him in the blink of an eye if she'd wanted by using her ability, though she probably didn't want to expose how fast she really was. Better for him. It meant as long as he stayed in the public eye, he could outpace her.

"Hey, asshole," Blade shouted. "I said wait."

Jayden froze, his hands balled into tight fists. When Blade's hand grabbed Jayden's shoulder from behind, Jay grabbed the guy's wrist, seething through his teeth. "I *really* want you to leave me alone right now."

A low laugh bubbled from Blade's chest. "You think you can tell me what to do?" As Jay turned to face him, Blade snapped his head forward and slammed right into Jayden's nose. The cracking of the bone-on-bone echoed in his ears. His head flew back and he stumbled, reaching for something to cling to as he fell. He caught a storm pipe and gripped it as hard as he could, blinking through blurred vision. He peered at the fuzzy figure of Blade, who walked toward him, clenching something shiny in his hand. A glint of light reflected off the sharp, steel surface.

If Jayden weren't already dead, he'd be worried. But the fact was, a knife—or any other weapon, for that matter—couldn't kill him.

The next fact was, if Blade stabbed him and Jay didn't bleed, Blade would know he wasn't exactly normal. And *that* would cause a problem. Maybe not so much for him, but for Hawa.

Jayden shook his head in an attempt to clear the receding fog from the edges of his sight. "Look, man." He stood upright, his vision finally cleared. "You just caught me on a bad day. I wasn't trying to start anything. I just want to be left alone."

The snake tattooed around Blade's biceps seemed to flex as he gripped the knife.

Jay's attention shifted over Blade's shoulder to Hawa, who stormed toward them, looking royally pissed. "Put it down, Blade." She passed him and stopped right in front of Jay. With black strands of hair hanging on either side of her sharp cheekbones, she pushed out her chin and glared. "Planning on ditching me, huh?" She shoved him in the chest. "I don't give a damn what you do or where you go. But don't you dare say a word about the Thirteenth Street Hotel, got it?" She jabbed her finger in his face. "These kids need this place, and—"

Jayden reached up and grabbed her wrist, and gently brought her hand down. "I won't say anything. I promise."

Hawa blinked. Her gaze flickered to his fingers pressed over her skin. Her throat tightened. "You're cold," she whispered.

Jayden let go of her. Of course, the only thing she'd notice about him was how he was different. He should be used to that by now. All his life he was always the black sheep. Too much of an asshole to get along with most guys, and too laid back to get along with most girls. Odd powers, and now being dead—kinda. He didn't fit anywhere.

Now, more than ever, he wished Zanya were still around to watch old Godzilla movies and eat junk food while they laughed at the actors in toothpaste commercials. But she wasn't, and even if things could go back to the way they were when they were friends, Zanya would never be his again. It was a fact he could live with, if he could just stop caring.

"Well, *I* say he can't go." Blade's voice broke Jayden out of his thoughts. With the knife still in his hand, Blade walked toward them and stopped beside Hawa. "You think just because you want to go means you can?" He scoffed and looked at Hawa. "You didn't tell this *gringo* anything about our place before you brought him here, did you?"

She returned his sharp glare. "Because he doesn't need to know, Blade. He's a guest."

Blade's gaze darkened and he trained his focus back to Jayden. "Na." He pointed the curved blade at Jayden. "He's more than that. I can tell." Blade poised the tip of the knife over Jay's heart.

Hawa smacked Blade's hand aside. "What the hell is your problem?"

Every muscle in Jayden's body tensed. It was clear Blade was some kind of badass around these parts, and Hawa defying him couldn't have been a good move. She'd said he'd kick her out. Excommunicate her, from whatever kind of fucked up community they had going. Or worse. Still, the kids in the hotel meant a lot to her, and Blade was bluffing. He had to be…

"I'm just going to go," Jayden said, taking a backward step. If he could get out of here fast enough, maybe it'd defuse the situation. "Like I said, I didn't mean to start—"

Blade lunged at Hawa and seized her throat. She immediately grabbed his forearm and tried to pull back, but he was too strong. "You think you're untouchable, *Brisa*? Think you're hot shit?"

"Hey!" Jayden leaped forward, stopping when Blade pressed a knife to Hawa's throat. Her eyes franticly searched his while her feet shifted on the sidewalk. He squeezed harder, pulling her onto her tiptoes.

"You have no businesses being back here," Blade said, his tone low and ominous. "Especially after what you did." Blade dragged the knife over her clothes, down to her belly. Hawa clutched harder onto his arm. "You are nothing but a murderer."

That's it.

Jayden swung his elbow and cracked Blade in the face. Blood gushed from his nose and he let go of Hawa's throat. She gasped and coughed, stumbling away until her back crashed against the brick wall of the Thirteenth Street Hotel.

She was okay, but he'd make damn sure nobody could say the same for the douche bag who thought it was okay to lay his hands on a woman.

Blade wiped blood from his face with the back of his hand, smearing a scarlet streak across his cheek. He raised his knife and grinned. "You're gonna die, *gringo*."

Jayden smirked. "Too late, asshole." He charged at Blade and slammed into him with a *Straight Outta Compton* front kick to the gut, knocking the air out of his lungs. Blade wheezed and forced himself to stand. He swiped the knife through the air, barely missing Jayden's stomach.

Jay jumped back with his hands positioned in front of him like a wrestler. Blade lunged again. Jay caught his hand and twisted his wrist, pointing the knife straight at Blade's chest.

"No!" Hawa appeared beside them in the blink of an eye. "Don't hurt him." She rested her hand on Jayden's shoulder. "The kids need him."

The heat bubbling in his chest fizzled, and the warmth from Hawa's touch brought his mind back to humanity. Her eyes searched his. Jayden curled his lip. "Fine, but only—"

Blade punched Jayden in the stomach—hard. Hawa gasped and let out a long chain of what he could only assume were curse words in Spanish. Jayden backed away and stared down at the handle of the dagger protruding from his side. Nobody spoke as he coiled his fingers around the handle and glanced up at Blade, who watched him intently. "Why the fuck did you go and do that?" Jayden grumbled.

Hawa rushed in front of Jayden and braced her hands on either of his shoulders. "You can't take it out. He'll know…"

Jayden observed Blade over her shoulder. The man stepped forward, his mouth slightly agape, his focus trained on him and Hawa.

Jay shook his head. "He already knows."

"What?"

"Does he know about *you*?" Jayden asked.

Hawa's features softened. "Um…"

"Why didn't you tell me?" Jayden's tone was sharper than he intended, but he couldn't help it. She should have told him someone knew about her. Especially this asshat.

"I'm sorry. I didn't think it was important. I…" Her bottom lip trembled—something that caught Jayden off guard. She wasn't the kind of girl to turn on the waterworks over just anything.

"So you're like her." Blade walked toward them. "You're different. How? Do you bleed? Are you made of metal or something?"

The stupidity of the question prompted both him and Hawa to exchange glances.

This guy's serious, Jay said with his mind. He took the handle of the knife, and in one swift motion, pulled it out. *Made of metal. What an idiot.*

"Shut up," Hawa whispered harshly.

When the knife was removed, he covered the wound with his hand.

Hawa immediately took the weapon from him. "Unlike you, *he'll* die if you stab him."

Blade stared at Jayden's wound, as if he were waiting for something. No blood seeped out to stain his shirt. He wouldn't fall to his knees in pain or have labored breathing. This was it. A hole in his side, no pain, and no way to heal from it. He'd have to learn how to avoid these things unless he wanted to be a human pincushion for the rest of his life.

Hawa frowned. "Come on. I need to stitch that up or…well, I have no idea what the hell will happen, but it doesn't seem right leaving it like that." Hawa turned and locked eyes with Blade. "If it's okay with you."

Blade paused, analyzed Jayden with a deep, calculating stare, and then nodded.

Jayden covered his broken nose with his fingers, and in one small move, cracked it back in place. Blade wouldn't have as easy a time with his. As they passed Blade, Jayden paused in front of him. "I don't give a fuck who you are, *Rico*. If you ever touch her again, I'll kill you." Jay let his hand fall away from the stab wound. "And there's nothing you can do to stop me."

CHAPTER EIGHT

"You can't go getting yourself stabbed like that," Hawa scolded while threading a needle with clear fishing line. The hotel room was dimly lit and the thin mattress on the floor was full of lumps—and possibly bedbugs—but that was as good as it was going to get.

"Yeah. I'll keep that in mind next time your crazy ex-boyfriend comes at me with a knife."

Hawa tied a knot in the fishing line and glanced up at him. "How do you know he's my ex?"

Jayden scoffed. "Kinda obvious, the way he looks at you. Like he thinks he owns you or something." He shifted his weight, staring at the huge needle pinched between her fingers. "That creeps me out."

"Blade thinks whatever he wants, right or wrong. Don't let him creep you out."

"No. Not him. The needle." He pushed his back against the wall. "I don't like them."

She gently lifted the hem of his shirt and winced at the sight of the gaping wound. "What do you have to be creeped out about? You have like a million tattoos. Those are done with needles." She poised the pointed tip over his skin. "At least this won't hurt, and it won't get infected…I don't think. I mean, if you can't die, you probably can't get sick either."

Jayden rested the back of his head against the wall and stared up at the ceiling. "That would be at least one perk."

"Just hold still."

Jayden pressed his eyes shut as she pushed the needle into his skin. No, it didn't hurt, but the fact he was being sewn up with an old needle and some fishing line still made his skin crawl. If he were still alive, he'd need a tetanus shot and a full course of antibiotics for sure.

When she finished, she cut the line with a par of dull scissors. "There. All done."

He stared down at the mended wound. "Not bad." And since the fishing line was clear, it almost unnoticeable. "Thanks."

Hawa's gaze didn't drift from his chest, and the intensity of her stare made Jayden shift his weight. She leaned in close to him and slipped her fingers under his shirt.

Jayden's breath hitched. "What are you doing?" His body temperature spiked—or at least it seemed that way. Another phantom reaction. Her fingertips dragged gently up his stomach until she reached the stitches put there by the hospital morgue after he was torn apart by Sarian.

She froze. Her lips parted. Jayden listened to her breathing, steady and rhythmic in the quiet room.

She bit her lip—something he'd never noticed her do before. Suddenly he was noticing a lot of things about her he never had.

Like her right iris had a fleck of gold in it that wasn't in the left one. Or the small scar on her chin. Or the fact that although she was normally a sarcastic pain the ass, there was another side to her. A side she hid. He just couldn't figure out why.

Hawa pushed to her knees. He instinctively lifted his hands as if surrendering. When she rested one leg to the other side of his body, straddling his waist, he parted his lips. "W—" He went silent at the sight of her searching gaze. He lifted his arms, allowing her to slip his shirt up over his head and toss it to the floor. A wave of humiliation rushed over him. She stilled and examined the crisscrossed stitches over his chest, and the once kick-ass tattoo job, now mangled and haphazardly pieced back together.

She traced her fingers along the mauled ink.

"I don't know if the scars will ever go away," he said softly.

She paused and rested her warm palm over his chest. "We all have scars. Some are just more visible than others." She swallowed, and her chest visibly fluttered.

With a whole hell of a lot of caution, he rested his hands gently over her hips. His fingers grazed the strip of midriff showing from under her t-shirt. She didn't flinch. Didn't pull away.

"Hawa..." Her name came out in a rough whisper.

Her lips curled into a sexy smile. "I don't think

I've ever heard you say my name before." Her cheeks flushed. "At least not like that."

He blinked, unsure how to react. "I…" She leaned forward, pressing her chest against his. "What are you doing?"

She pressed her index finger over her lips, and then traced her hands down his arms.

His breath picked up. There was no denying he was turned on. It had been longer than he cared to admit since he had some action. But there was also no denying he wished it was Zanya pressed against his body instead of her.

He rested his hands on her shoulders, holding her inches away. "I can't do this." He looked away. "I'm sorry."

"Don't be sorry." She ran her fingers through his hair. His eyes fluttered shut. The gentleness in her touch overwhelmed him. It was a shock anything about her could be gentle. "Neither of us should be sorry. We haven't done anything wrong. And now we can help each other."

Jayden drew his eyebrows together and opened his eyes. "What do you mean?"

"We're both hurting. You for Zanya. Me…" She dropped her head. "For a lifetime of shitty decisions."

Without realizing it, his hands had drifted around her back and his fingers were curled around her waist.

She glanced down at the zipper of his jeans. "Do you think everything still works?" She cocked an eyebrow.

Jayden's eyes widened. "I…" He hadn't thought

about it until now. No blood flow meant bad things for his love life.

"We can find out." She rolled her hips.

A low moan rose through his chest. He swallowed against a dry throat. "I sure as hell hope it does."

Hawa brushed her lips over is. Her hot breath crashed against his mouth. He returned her kiss, barely, still not sure if this was what he wanted. Would doing this mean he was betraying Zanya? It seemed that way. He'd lived so long totally dedicated to her. But the reality was, she had moved on, and he would eventually have to accept that.

Maybe the sprinter was right. Maybe they could help each other.

He savored the weight of her body on top of his as she wound her legs tighter around him. He ran his hands down her thighs, curling his fingers around solid muscle. "Wait." He blinked open his eyes. "I don't have any protection."

She slid her hand in the back pocket of her jeans and pulled out a square foil wrapper with a circular ring on the inside of the packaging. "Just in case."

***

Jayden awoke in a dark space. He was fully dressed, which was not the case when he went to sleep. And there was nothing around him. Absolutely nothing. He turned one way, and then the other. "Um...hello?"

Of course. He had to be dreaming. He walked into the darkness in search of whatever his twisted subconscious came up with. As he walked, the space just kept going, with nothing but silence to greet him. He stopped. "Hello?" His voice echoed into the emptiness. He cupped his hands around his mouth and shouted louder. "Hello?"

"You don't have to scream."

Jayden spun and spotted Modem standing a few yards away. The spunky girl with neon sweatbands on either wrist and multi-colored necklaces grinned. How weird he was dreaming about her. Creepy, actually. "Um...hey." He nodded. "What's up?"

Modern scoffed and rolled her eyes. "You really are as dense as you look, aren't you?"

Jayden blinked. "What?"

"What?" she mimicked.

"Hey. Knock it off."

"Hey. Knock it off." She rested her hands on her hips.

He exhaled and walked in the opposite direction. "I don't need this right now. I have enough shit to deal with without having an annoying kid in my dreams."

"Dreams?" Quick footsteps grew louder until she reached his side and fell into pace. She shoved her hands into her pockets and stared up at him. "You think you're dreaming?"

"What else could this be?" He turned left, then right. "Hey, do you know how to get out of here?"

"Um, yeah. But I doubt you want to do that."

He paused. "Yeah, actually. I do."

She rocked forward on her toes and back onto her heels. "I really don't think you want to. Better off staying here, with me."

He slouched his shoulders. "Just about anything is better than staying here with you."

She stopped rocking and frowned. "Fine. But don't say I didn't warn you. Jerk." She walked off, her tiny frame devoured by the darkness.

"I have no idea why Hawa likes that girl," he mumbled.

The roar of rushing water caught Jayden's attention, and he spun to see a tidal wave charging him. He shouted and threw up his hands as a shield, but it was no use. The wall of water plowed into him like a wrecking ball and slammed him against the floor. It rushed up his nose and into his throat. He kicked and reached for the surface, but the water was moving too fast. Just when he couldn't hold his breath any longer, the wave receded and settled into a puddle beneath him. He coughed and sputtered liquid from his lungs.

Bright light assaulted his eyes. He squinted into the distance—nothing but desert and abandoned Mayan temples in every direction.

Contessa's silky voice carried over the barren land. Jayden jumped to his feet and peered to the far temple where she stood, book propped in her hands, her eyes inked into black wells of onyx.

She whispered in a foreign language. Her words were harsh and grew in intensity between each breath. His stomach cramped. The air seemed to thicken. Contessa's red waves of hair floated off her shoulders, splaying around her as if gravity did not exist.

Bits of soil fell over his shoulders. He raised his

face to the sky, where roots from an enormous tree writhed and whipped wildly above him. He'd seen the tree before, but this time it seemed...angry. The sight nearly knocked him on his ass. He stumbled back and dragged his steps over the dry ground, stirring clouds of dust.

A soft laugh tinkled through the air.

Jayden froze, unable to shake the prickling sensation crawling over his skin.

That Modem kid was right. This couldn't be a dream. No dream was this realistic.

A hand grabbed his foot, and Jayden leaped back.

Hands. Thousands of hands with broken fingernails and bloody knuckles reached from beneath the earth and clawed to the surface. Raw skin peeled away, exposing tendon and bone. Jayden leaped onto the bottom step of a nearby temple and watched as the ground of this godforsaken land writhed with reaching hands, like maggots in a bloated corpse.

Jayden's eyes shot open and he sat up in bed. Hawa blinked, her bare shoulders exposed from under the blanket covering them both. "You okay?" Her voice was sleep-laden and soft.

"Um..." He was back in the hotel room with Hawa. Back under the covers, lying beside her where he had drifted off to sleep in the middle of the day, just a few hours ago. "I think so. I had a really weird dream." He ran his fingers through his hair, leaving wild strands to hang down around his face.

Hawa rolled over and tucked the blankets under her arms, covering her chest. "Contessa?"

He stared down at her. "How did you know?"

"An obvious guess." Her black hair feathered over the pillow. A strip of bright sunlight pushing through the curtains streaked over her face. She smiled.

Damn. She really was beautiful when she smiled.

"She was doing something with the book."

Hawa pushed up onto her elbow. "What?"

Jayden examined her for a moment. Her skin carried a soft glow, and the dark circles under her eyes were nearly gone. The rest had been good for her, and weighing her mind down with worries about Contessa would only lay on another layer of stress. "You know what, I'll tell you about it later." He pulled Hawa closer to him and groaned. "Can we just sleep for the rest of the day?" Her cheek nestled in the curve of his shoulder. It was a welcomed change to have someone lying beside him. She shivered, and Jay frowned. "I'm sorry." He tucked the blanket around her so she wasn't touching his bare chest. "I don't mean to make you cold. Can't really help it."

She curled into a ball. "That's okay. I'm used to being cold. Spent enough time here cold at night."

"I thought you had electricity."

She curled into a tighter ball. "Heat runs off of gas, and that's not so easy to borrow."

"Steal, you mean."

She shrugged with a soft smile.

He chuckled and threw the covers off him, careful not to tear them off her too. "I'm going to—" Telling her his vision now included Modem would probably just freak her out. "I'll be back."

She sat up, clutching the blanket to her body. "You going to try to take off again?"

He shook his head. "I'll stick around." He stood and slipped on his pants. "For a while at least."

She snorted and threw his shirt at him. "Like every man in the world—quick to get dressed."

He laughed. "It's not like that."

He had to talk to the kid. Something told him she knew way more than she pretended. And now that she was stalking around in his visions, it was up to him to find out why.

CHAPTER NINE

Jayden had searched the hotel from top to bottom, in every room, on every staircase. No annoying little girl. He even stopped by the room full of computer parts where she spent most of her time. Nothing.

He stood in the center of the lobby, arms crossed, leaning against the dry stone fountain. "Hey." Hawa walked toward him with a mop and broom in one hand, and a half-filled bucket of water in the other. "We need to do chores."

"Oh." He stood up straight. "Really?" He eyed a puddle on the floor nearby collecting drops from a leak in the roof. "This place needs serious work, and then maybe a deep cleaning."

She set down the supplies. "Yes, I see that. But I can't turn back time and keep this place from falling apart, so cleaning is the best we can do." She handed him the mop. "I'll sweep, you follow with the mop."

Jayden stood in silence, watching Hawa gather dust and dirt into a pile while the walls around her were bowed, the floors were splintered, and the ceiling was probably a few years away from caving in.

"You're kidding, right?"

She responded by pushing a pile of dirt into a dustpan and emptying it into a plastic bag. "Are you going to help or just stand there?" She hadn't made eye contact with him since she came downstairs, and her posture was stiff. "We have to get this done before we can have anything to eat. Those are the rules." When he didn't reply, she stopped sweeping and finally looked at him. "*What*?"

He leaned on the mop. "So…is this going to be weird now?" When she didn't respond, he frowned. "Hawa."

She pursed her lips. "It won't get weird if you don't make it weird. So just…don't, okay?" She returned to sweeping. "We both needed something. We gave it to each other. That's it."

Just a few hours ago, she'd been someone completely different. Her eyes warm, her lips soft against his. Her touch was gentle, and he could have sworn she felt something. That she wanted to be with him. It was the first time in months he'd had a connection with anyone…or so he'd thought.

He dipped the mop in a bucket of water and slopped it over the floor, following where she had swept. And that was it. Sweep and mop. Sweep and mop. More awkward silence.

About a half hour later, Jayden dropped the mop in the bucket and sloshed it around, watching Hawa collect the last of the dirt pile. *I never knew you had a domestic streak in you,* he said with his mind.

"I don't." She glanced back at him. "Now shut up before—"

"Hey!" A girl's voice called from above them.

Jayden stopped and peered up to the second floor. Modem stood with her hands on her hips, staring down at him. "You gonna make me wait all day?"

Hawa turned toward him. "What is she talking about?"

Jayden shrugged. "I don't know."

"Why does she want to talk to you?"

He rested the mop against the wall and walked toward the staircase. "Don't know," he lied. "I'll go see." He scaled the stairs to where Modem waited, her four-foot-two frame standing way taller in attitude than someone her age should be allowed.

"Like I said. Dense." Modem turned and waved Jayden forward. "Come on. We need to talk."

Jayden followed her into an empty room, where she shut and locked the door before climbing out the only window, onto a fire escape. She bent over, peering back into the room at him. "You coming or what?" A warm breeze swept into the room, blowing strands of her curly black hair around her face.

He glanced over his shoulder. Hawa could be on her way up. Better to talk to the brat without her around, which meant getting out of the hotel. Even if he wasn't totally fond of heights.

He threw one leg out the window, and then the other. The rusted steel of the fire escape groaned under his weight. Modem was already halfway down the ladder leading to a narrow street. He grabbed hold of the railing and peered over the edge. "Is this really necessary?"

Modem stopped and looked up. *You want Brisa to follow us? Because she will if she knows we went out the main entrance.*

Jayden's lips parted. Hot shit. She did it too—the whole mind-talking thing.

Who was this girl?

"Okay, then," he mumbled before following her down. The sounds of the city filled his ears— honking horns, the rush of cars zooming by, and the low, steady murmur of people talking on their cellphones as they walked down the sidewalks.

"Where are we going?" He strode beside Modem, and she kicked a pebble along the way, watching it bounce until it came to a stop. "Hey. Why didn't you tell me you were like us?"

Modem shrugged. "'Cause." She stole a glance at him, and then rolled her eyes. "Brisa would have freaked out if she found out, okay?"

"She doesn't know?"

"Nope. And I'm not going to tell her, either. Not yet, anyway."

"Why?"

"Because she's overprotective and crazy."

Jayden grinned. The girl was growing on him. "What were you doing in my dream last night?"

"In your dreams?" She kicked the pebble again. This time it flew into the bushes. "You some kinda perv or something?"

His eyes widened. "What? No, I didn't—"

She laughed. "I'm just messing with you." She turned a corner, leading him down a thin walkway to what looked like a park set in the center of the city. Towering trees gave shade to kids on swings and a few women sitting at a picnic table.

Modem twirled a few strands of hair around her finger. "What are you doing here, really?"

Jayden shrugged. "I don't know. Hawa brought us here. What are *you* doing here? You're not like the other kids."

"Clearly. And I knew you were like Brisa the second I saw you. That you guys were the same—had some kind of ability, like me." She slowed beside a low rock wall and hopped onto the edge, dangling her feet off the side.

Jayden plopped beside her. "So…you're Riyata, too?"

Modem blinked at him. "Is that what you call it?" She chewed on her bottom lip. "I always felt like a total freak until Hawa came along. When I found out what she could do, I didn't feel so weird."

"Why didn't you say anything when we got here?"

"I guess 'cause I don't trust you. Maybe I wasn't sure." She fidgeted with one of her necklaces.

"Fair enough." Neither of them spoke while they watched the people in the park. They were all so carefree, laughing and playing in the late-afternoon heat.

"Why do you keep looking for that woman?"

Jayden shook his head. "I'm a seeker, it's kind of what I do. But I don't seek her. Not on purpose, anyway. My ability has been kind of schizo lately." He tapped his temple with his finger. "It's all messed up. I can't control it."

"Oh. Well, that makes sense. I wondered if you had some kind of death wish or something." Modem shook her head, her tiny features carrying more concern than most kids would understand. "That lady is bad news. I can feel it."

"Yeah. I know." He plucked a yellow weed out of the grass and spun it between his fingers. "So, what do you do, anyway? Read minds?"

"I'm a hacker. The best hacker—"

"Between here and Fifty-Fourth Street. Yeah, I remember."

"Right. I hack into dreams, thoughts, and memories."

"Reminds me of this creepy girl from back where I stayed before this." Freaking *Children-of-the-Corn* Marzena and her mind powers. Could Modem be a dreamwalker? It explained why Modem liked computers so much. Dreamwalkers preferred to be alone. Hacking computer systems was a one-person job, and she spent a ton of time fiddling around with all of the flashing lights, alone in her room tucked in a quiet corner of the hotel.

"Hey. How old are you?"

Model eyed him. "Twelve. Why?"

"Twelve, twelve? Or fourteen hundred, twelve?"

She furrowed her brow. "Are you on drugs?"

He scratched his head. "You should probably talk to Hawa when we get back." Apparently, Modem didn't know what the whole dreamwalker thing consisted of. The poor kid still didn't know she wouldn't age much more, no matter how old she was. Of course nobody had really confirmed it yet, but from what he had seen, his theory was pretty solid.

"Okay." She stretched out the word. "Anyway, where were you before you came here?"

"Doesn't matter." His thoughts flashed to Zanya. "Not anymore." He tossed the weed to the ground, determined to stop doing that—stop thinking about her at random times, when he wasn't prepared and it hurt him the most. "So," he continued. "You hacked into my dream and blocked Contessa from seeing me?"

"Pretty much. Who is she?"

"A witch. She's powerful, and she's using that book to do something *really* not good." The image of hands reaching up through the soil flashed through his mind.

"So the book is important?"

Jayden nodded. "It has a bunch of Mayan history in it and is loaded with important stuff that needs to be kept safe."

Over the next hour, he tried to explain everything to the girl with as much honesty as he could, while not making it sound too scary. There was no telling how much she could handle. But the fact was, it was a matter of life or death. Contessa wouldn't waste her time on small stuff. If she succeeded at whatever she was up to, it would be bad news for everyone. Including the kid.

"Then I guess we don't have a choice," Modem said. "I'll help you get it back." She hopped off the ledge and walked back toward the hotel.

"Wait. What?" He followed her down the walkway. "No way. It would be too dangerous."

She blew out a puff of air. "Yeah, 'cause you did

a peachy job keeping yourself out of trouble last time, didn't'cha? Face it. You need me. If you wanna get that book, you need me to hack into your seeker-vision-thing and keep her from knowing you're snooping around. Then you can get close enough to snatch the book."

He had to admit, the kid had a good idea. He pressed his lips into a tight line. "Hawa would kill me."

"She doesn't have to know. Not unless you tell her."

Jayden walked in silence, considering her proposition. She could come in handy. Then again, she could get herself killed.

"What's up with you and Brisa, anyway? You guys dating?"

Jayden shrugged. "No." He paused. "I don't know. Maybe."

She snorted. "Doesn't sound like you are if you don't know."

"It's complicated. What's going on between her and Blade?"

Modem crinkled her nose. "She didn't tell you?"

"It's obvious they were a thing, but past that, I didn't ask."

"I'll tell you, but only if you swear not to tell her I told you, 'cause she'd be really mad."

"Okay, sure."

"Seriously. I don't trust you. If you want me to, you have to earn it."

He drew an X over his chest and lifted two fingers. "Boy Scout's honor."

Modem rolled her eyes. "It's three fingers,

genius." She chuckled. "Anyway, so yeah, they used to be a thing. *The* thing, actually. It was a lot better back then. The hotel was kept in pretty good shape thanks to Brisa being on top of everything. She looked after the kids—like, really looked after them. She cared about what they ate and found a way to get them to the public clinic if they were sick. It was like having a big sister who was a local badass. But she was *always* by Blade's side, no matter what. The rules were enforced, but not with fear, like they are now. And nobody ever went missing or got kicked out." Her eyes saddened. "Not like now. Her and Blade ran the place together. After Brisa lost the baby, he never forgave her, and she took off."

Jayden stopped mid-stride. "Baby?" he said softly.

Modem's face drained of color. "You didn't know that either?"

He shook his head.

She clapped her hand over her mouth.

"Hawa was pregnant?"

Model let her hand fall to her side. "Please don't tell her I told you. Since you guys are dating—maybe—I figured you knew."

"I won't tell her, but..." Fuck. How did he even respond to that?

"Listen." She shifted toward him. "It wasn't her fault. They were both shocked when she found out she was pregnant. Blade was happy. Hawa, not so much. When she lost it, he blamed her. He said she never wanted it in the first place. But she didn't do what he thinks she did." The girl balled her fists.

"He never should have shoved her that hard." Her eyes darkened. "She broke right through the railing."

A spike of rage tore through Jayden's gut. "What?" He worked his jaw. "He hit her?"

Modem looked away. "More than that." She swallowed. "It was bad." She crossed her arms, seeming more like a little girl in that moment. "After she got out of the hospital, Brisa left, and we didn't hear from her again, until she came back with you."

CHAPTER TEN

Jayden walked along the narrow alleyway, toward the dead neon sign, and through the side door, straight into the hotel. No knocking. No secret password. Enough was enough.

In the main foyer, he spotted Hawa standing with her shoulders hunched, slopping the soggy mop over cracked tile and tattered wooden floor. She wiped her forehead with the back of her hand and glanced up, spotting him. "Where the hell have you been?"

"Out." He walked past her, toward the stairs.

"With Modem?" She tossed the mop at him. The handle smacked him in the head and bounced off, clattering to the floor.

"What do you care?"

"Because you have chores to do, asshole." She gestured to the puddle on the floor. "I got stuck pulling your load."

He squared his shoulders. "*My load*? You're talking to me like this is my home. Like I give a shit if Blade or anyone else around here says I need to do chores, which is the definition of *fucking stupid* in a place that's falling apart." He kicked the pail of water, throwing it feet away and splashing dirty water in every direction. With his jaw clenched, he shook his head. "Who are you? This isn't the Hawa I knew in Renato's house. You were always so hard and confident. You're not the same when you're here." He wanted to tell her he knew about the baby, and about her putting up with Blade beating on her like his personal punching bag. He wanted to shake her by the shoulders and demand she explain herself—why she'd put up with that bullshit when she could have fought back.

Hawa shifted her weight, her eyes averted to the floor. "What did Modem tell you?"

"It doesn't matter."

"It matters," she said in a low growl.

It doesn't change anything, he said with his mind.

Hawa nodded, and her lips turned down in to a frown. "It changes a lot."

"Brisa!"

Hawa jumped, and looked up to the third floor. Blade leaned against the railing, staring down at them.

Hawa cleared her throat. "Yeah?"

He waved her up. "Come here a minute."

She stole a glance at Jayden, and then nodded. "Sure. Be right there."

Not alone, you're not.

"Stay out of it," she whispered as she passed him.

He watched her scale the stairs. *Have we met?*

He tailed her just close enough so he could hear what was going on, but not too close to draw any attention.

When she reached the third floor, Jayden slowed his pace and spied between the rusted railings.

When Blade draped his arm over her shoulder, Hawa's muscles tensed under his touch.

"What's going on?" Blade said in a low, steady voice.

She squirmed, clearly trying to shift his arm off her shoulders without being too forceful. "What do you mean?"

He calmly brushed her hair away from her neck with the other hand. She cringed.

"Is there something going on I should know about?" he asked.

She shrugged. "Just finishing my chores."

"Right." He analyzed her face. "And you and the *gringo*. What about that? Something going on there?"

She paused, and her eyes narrowed. "We're just traveling together. I told you."

He let out a low laugh. "Kind of like how you and me were just traveling together, huh?"

"No. Not like that." She stepped back.

His arm slid off her shoulders, and he pumped his fists. "No? Not like that?" He stepped closer, pinning her back against the wall.

"Blade—"

He rested a hand on either side of her, trapping her in place. "I missed the way you say my name, you know that?"

Jayden crept up a step as silently as he could. If

he had to step in, things would get ugly.

"I need to go finish my chores," Hawa said. Her voice carried a slight tremble.

"Say my name again. Just one more time." Blade shifted even closer to her, pressing his body against hers. He pinched her face between his fingers, puckering her lips.

Hawa sucked in a breath and jerked her head to the side. "Stop it, Blade."

He grinned. "That wasn't so hard, was it?" He dragged his fingers down her cheek. "I really did miss you, Brisa." He grabbed her face again and forced his lips against hers.

Jayden ground his teeth. That was it.

When he stepped toward them, a shooting pain tore through his temples. He crumbled to the stairs and cupped his hands over his ears, squinting his eyes shut.

The black space opened up to him, and Modem appeared behind his closed lids, in his subconscious. "You don't want to do that." She cocked her head to the side, pursing her lips.

Jayden stood in the void space with the girl. "Get out of my head."

"You were about to do something stupid. I'm saving you. You could say thank you."

"He's hurting her."

"What, are you her babysitter or something? Brisa has been dealing with Blade for as long as I can remember. If you step in, it'll just make it worse."

"Not if I kill him first," he said through clenched teeth.

"And then what'll happen to all the kids who live in the Thirteenth Street Hotel? You plan to take care of us when Blade is gone?"

Jayden snorted. He could barely take care of himself.

"Don't forget, your powers are different now. That's why I gave you the ability to talk to her with your mind." She tapped her head.

Jayden searched for a logical explanation, and came up with only one. It was her. She was the reason he could talk to Hawa with his mind.

Modem's eyes widened and her lips parted, showing a faint smile. "You thought you were doing that by yourself?" She laughed. Like, a full on belly laugh. Little jerk. "Okay. Here's the deal." She shifted toward him. "I'm helping you out because you're helping Brisa. So as long as you're here, with her, I'll keep letting you *borrow* the ability to talk to her through your mind." She quoted the word 'borrow' with her fingers.

"And if I leave?"

"You go back to your ability controlling you, and nobody there to help when the crazy witch decides she's going to eat your brains." She shrugged. "Everyone's got to pay some kind of price, right?"

He narrowed his eyes. "Are you sure you're only twelve? Like, legit twelve?"

Her brow furrowed again. "You've got to stop asking stupid questions. What other kind of twelve is there?" She rolled her eyes. "Just shut up and don't do anything stupid. Brisa is a big girl. She can handle Blade, as long as you don't make it harder for her. Meanwhile, you and I have a witch to hunt."

***

After his splitting headache subsided, Jayden wove through the hotel to Modem's computer room. The door hung open, showing a labyrinth of blinking lights, crisscrossed cords, and computer monitors, all displaying endless lines of green code scrolling over the screen. He stepped inside and shut the door behind him.

Modem looked at him from the corner, half-buried in disassembled computer parts. "Hey."

"Oh. Hi." It would take some time to get used to meeting up with a kid. But he'd seen what Marzena could do, and Modem was formidable. She just wore the ability a lot different, though that was probably due to her genuine youth.

"So, here's what I'm thinking," she said, typing away at a keyboard. "You need that book, right?"

Jayden nodded. "She's using it to do…" He scratched the back of his head. What she was doing with the book, exactly, he wasn't sure. But it wasn't good. "Stuff."

Modem paused and gazed up at him with an unamused stare. "Stuff," she stated flatly. She gave a long exhale and returned her gaze to the computer screen. "We don't know where Contessa is hiding, doing this *stuff*, right?"

"Not unless we want to try our luck in Moscow, where she lives."

"Na." Modem tossed a handful of green and

silver computer chips in the garbage. "I doubt she's stupid enough to stay there with the book, now that she knows you're onto her."

"What makes you think she knows?"

Modem snorted. "Thanks to your ability going rogue, I'm pretty sure she spotted you the first time you sought her. Or she at least has a clue."

He nodded and shoved his hands in his pockets. "Right. I forgot about that."

"That place you find her looks pretty nasty, if you ask me. The desert and all those hands coming out of the ground."

How did she know about that? She wasn't protecting him then, but she must have still been spying on his vision. Jayden froze. That vision was right after he and Hawa…"Okay. Ground rules." He stepped toward her, staring down at her tiny frame. "No climbing in my head unless we agree on it. There's stuff I want to keep…personal."

She pursed her lips. "Yeah, sure. Personal." She nodded. "Got it."

"I'm serious."

"I know." She raised her hand, lifting her index and middle finger together. "Girl Scout's honor." She grinned.

The girl was clever. He'd have to be doubly cautious around her. "So what's your master plan?" A part of him couldn't believe he was asking a kid that question.

"Do that seeky thing you do again, and this time, I'll stay with you the entire time. We'll figure out exactly where she is, find out how to get there *for real*, and not just in a vision, and then we'll take that book.”

“I doubt that’s possible.”

“Why?”

“Because where she’s hiding isn’t really anywhere we can go. Not physically, anyway.”

Modem’s fingers stilled over the keyboard and she peered up at him. “What does that mean?”

Telling the kid about the underworld, and the fact he’d had an extended stay there once, was a little more info than he cared to share. Maybe just giving her half the truth was good enough for now. “She’s hiding in another realm.”

Curiosity flickered in her gaze. “Really?” A half-smile spread over her lips. “Where? There are other realms? How do you go there? Why is she—?”

“Whoa.” He snickered. “One question at a time, and not so many, if you don’t mind.”

“But I want to know—”

“I know you do. There’s probably a lot you want to know, but you shouldn’t try to learn it all at once. It’s a lot to wrap your mind around.”

She was silent a moment, and then groaned. “Fine.”

“Fine.” He smiled softly. Poor kid had a lifetime of learning about a world she never imagined existed. First, they needed to take care of Contessa, and then they’d have some free time to tell the girl about her future. His smile faded. A future as a kid, forever. “Okay.” He cleared his throat. “So I’m thinking if we follow your plan with a few tweaks, we can still get this done. I’ll seek her, you protect me, and I’ll grab the book.”

“What makes you think you can take it through a

vision? Does it work like that?"

Considering the hands that had grabbed his ankles had left scratches, and the heat really did scorch his skin, just about anything was possible. "I think so." His mind flickered to Zanya and the danger she'd be in if he didn't at least stall Contessa from completing her plan. "I hope so."

"First things first." She crossed her arms. "What's in it for me?"

Jayden examined her closely. The kid was up to something. "What do you want?"

She shrugged. "That's easy. Out of here."

He stepped aside and gestured to the door. "Want me to open it for you?"

"No, idiot. Out of this hotel. I'm sick of living in this place with all these people. I don't have any privacy, and there's no way I'm going into the system. But Brisa used to tell me about her uncle's house when she went to visit. It sounds pretty nice over there."

"I won't stand in your way from moving there tomorrow. They'd probably welcome you in, but you'll have to go alone. I'm not going back."

"Really." The word was more of a statement than a question. "What about Brisa? You're just going to let her leave when she decides to go home?"

"I don't know if she's going back. But like you said. If she does, she can take care of herself."

Modem examined him, and then curled her lip. "You *are* a jerk. Forget it. I don't want to help." She sat back and picked up another stack of computer chips, analyzing each of them, one at a time.

"So that's it?" He waited, but she didn't respond.

"You can't just pretend you're not different. That you're not like us."

Modem shrugged. "I have no idea what you're talking about. I'm just a kid."

"How about I ask Hawa if she knows what I'm talking about?"

Modem lifted her gaze. "You wouldn't."

"You don't know me very well."

Her lips parted. "You *would*."

"She's gotta find out sometime." He shrugged. "You know what they say. There's no time like the present."

She stood, watching him in silence from across the room. Her features sobered as her chest rose and fell and her breaths quickened. "You can't tell her." Her tone was low and steady.

Jayden's grin slowly vanished.

Modem's normally honey brown eyes darkened into murky pools, like Marzena's had when she helped fight off the incubi on the beach at Renato's home.

"Whoa." Jayden shifted away. "Calm down."

Hundreds of computer chips rose from the ground and hovered in the air, spinning in slow, threatening circles.

Jayden lifted his hands. "Modem. Chill out."

"You can't tell her," she whispered again. The air rippled with energy.

"I get that now. I won't tell her. Just…" His gut twisted into a knot and he scanned the room, spotting an open window on the other side. "Just calm down."

Modem continued to mumble, as if she couldn't

hear him.

The computer chips froze.

The air grew stale and silence draped over the room, ringing in his ears.

Jayden leaped toward the window, finding his exit just before the legion of shimmering metal chips shot through the air, and lodged into the door like daggers.

CHAPTER ELEVEN

That night, Jayden sat in the dark hotel room, his back propped against the wall. Hawa slept on the lumpy mattress across from him, curled under a blanket. He couldn't stop watching her. There was something about how her features softened while she slept. It was entrancing, in a non-stalker kind of way.

The hotel was surprisingly quiet for housing so many kids, and the city soundtrack outside was oddly soothing. Car alarms blared, drunks shouted in Spanish in the streets, and cars swooshed as they drove past. It all mixed into white noise, lulling the orphans in the Thirteenth Street Hotel to sleep.

Jayden pushed to his feet and walked to the room's single window. Not having to sleep at night was cool, but much more boring than he'd ever imagined. People always said, "If I had more hours in the day, I'd do so much more."

What a sack of shit.

Anyone he'd ever cared about had either forgotten about him completely, or was asleep at night, leaving him alone with his thoughts. Maybe he'd go back to the way things should be and try to sleep while the rest of the world stayed true to nature's rhythm.

He looked over his shoulder at Hawa. She had barely spoken to him since they'd spent the night together. Things *had* gotten weird.

Jayden frowned.

What wasn't weird anymore?

Her chest rose and fell with every breath. Strands of black hair were feathered over her cheek. Her lips were full and softly parted.

She was beautiful in the wildest of ways. Snark and indifference hid the glimpses of endearment he caught when she smiled. He still couldn't quite figure her out.

Hawa drew in a deep breath and turned onto her side to face him. Her lips curled into a faint smile. "You think I'm beautiful," she said very matter-of-factly.

He turned to face her, resting his back against the wall. "You heard me." His response mirrored her tone.

She pulled the blanket under her chin. "You think really, really loud."

Fantastic. "I'll try to keep my thoughts to myself."

It'd be a lie if he said he wasn't bitter. They'd had a hot night together that somehow made him hurt a little less over losing Zanya, and then she acted like nothing had happened between them. But something *did* happen, and he couldn't shake the memory of her soft, olive skin, her lips dominating his, and the way she fearlessly dove into him. He couldn't stop remembering, and he couldn't stop wanting more.

Jayden's throat tightened.

Hawa frowned. "I didn't know it was like that."

So much for keeping his thoughts to himself. He stared out the window. Anything to avert his gaze. "It's not," he lied.

"Thoughts don't lie."

"Too bad I can't read yours." The words came out sharp and full of animosity.

She sat up and watched him. "It's just…nobody's ever thought of me like that before."

"What, beautiful? I'm pretty sure Blade does." He was still pissed over Modem stepping in when all Jay wanted to do was instill the fear of God into that douche bag. One thing was for sure, whether kid intruded in his mind or not, if Blade ever put his hands on Hawa again, it'd be the last time.

"Blade doesn't care about me. Not really." She gathered the blanket in her hands and twisted the fabric.

His chest tightened. "You don't have to let him treat you like that. He acts like he owns you."

"That's just how Blade is. He's had a rough life, and he's responsible for this place. For the kids."

"Don't give me that bullshit." Jay clenched his jaw. "You were responsible for this place once too. You know this place isn't good for them anymore, but you don't do shit about it. You could fight the way he treats you. I've seen you do it everywhere else, with *everyone*. Maybe that's why Peter couldn't—" He hung his head. Fuck.

Hawa nodded. "Yeah." Her breath quivered. "Maybe."

Jayden ran his fingers through his hair and he pursed his lips. "I didn't mean—"

"No. It's okay. You're probably right. But fighting is the only reason I made it this far." She dropped her gaze and shrugged. "Why do you think I left this place? I couldn't take it anymore. This hotel was my home, but after…" Hawa brushed her fingers down her belly. He wouldn't have thought anything of it if he didn't already know.

"It's not your home anymore." He crouched beside her, meeting her face to face. "Let's get out of here."

Her eyebrows drew together. "Leave?"

"Yeah. Why not? You don't owe this place anything, and you've been miserable since we got here. Let's just go."

"Where?"

"Who cares?" He reached out and brushed strands of hair away from her face. He skimmed his thumb along the side of her mouth and cradled her cheek. "Anywhere."

She swallowed, her features filling with anxiety.

He let his hand fall away. "You're still in love with him."

She snorted. "No. Not even close."

"Then what?"

Her shoulders tensed.

"Hawa."

"Forget about it." She lay back down and pulled the covers around her shoulder. "Just go back to sleep."

"You can't do that." She didn't respond. "Damn it, Hawa." He stood, staring down at her. "You have some serious fucking issues, you know that?"

"Yeah." She sniffled. "Yeah, I know."

The heat coiling his muscles cooled. He ground his teeth, searching for something to say. Something to make her open up to him. Something to make him mean something to her.

"You can go," she said softly. "I won't be mad, and I won't judge. I'm sorry I brought you here."

His breath stalled. "You want me to leave?"

After a moment of silence, she answered in a mere whisper. "No."

Jayden shifted his weight, and then held out his hand.

She examined it in a moment of silence.

He wouldn't pull away. He waited, his hand outstretched in the stuffy, shadowed room.

Hawa sat up, analyzing him. A tear rolled down her cheek. She quickly brushed it away.

He shifted, still waiting.

She pursed her lips and swallowed.

As he began to curl his fingers, she took his hand and pushed to her feet.

He pulled her close, brushing his body against hers. "I thought you were going to leave me hanging there for a second."

She bit her lip through a smile, and her arms wound around his neck. "Yeah. I was thinking about it." She buried her fingers in his hair.

For the first time since he left the orphanage, his heart wasn't tied to Zanya. Now, in this moment, his heartache took a new form. He wanted the sprinter in a fierce way, for reasons he didn't understand. Something about her drew him in. Made him want to stay. Need to stay, if she'd have him.

Hawa nodded. "Yes."

He leaned in closer. "Yes, what?" He needed to hear her say it, even if he already knew.

She coiled her fingers around handfuls of his hair. Hot tension wound in his muscles.

"Yes," she whispered again, her breath breaking over his lips. "I'll have you."

He claimed her mouth, kissing her hard and deep. His tongue glided over hers, and he wound his hands around the back of her waist, then lifted her up. She hugged his torso with her legs. He stepped forward and slammed her back against the wall, somewhat surprised they didn't put a gaping hole in it.

Hawa let out a tiny moan and pinched his bottom lip between her teeth. He crushed her against his chest as her fingers trailed down the sides of his ribs and hooked around the buckle of his belt. A groan crawled up his throat.

"Jay," she said in a quick breath.

He pulled away, just enough to look her in the eyes.

"I..." She swallowed. "I should tell you something first. Before we go down this road."

He pressed another kiss on her lips. Sweeter this time. "I know."

She braced her hands on his shoulders. "Know what, exactly?"

"Don't be mad at Modem. She didn't mean to

tell me. It just slipped out." He dragged his gaze down to her belly, and let out a deep sigh. "It must have been really hard for you." He cradled her cheek. "I won't let anything else happen to you. Not like that. Not ever again."

***

Hey. Modem's voice barged into Jayden's mind, waking him out of a deep sleep.

Jayden groaned and blinked open his eyes. *What the hell do you want? I'm sleeping.*

I thought you couldn't sleep.

Jayden signed. *I can. I just don't have to.*

Wanna catch a bite to eat? I know this great diner a few blocks away. They have pie.

Jayden's stomach growled. Great. Now he was hungry. He checked on Hawa, who was still lying asleep beside him. It'd be at least another couple of hours until sunrise. He could slip out, gorge on some food, grab Hawa something for breakfast, and be back before she knew he was gone.

Is this your way of apologizing for trying to kill me earlier?

Who said I was sorry?

He pursed his lips.

Stop pouting and come outside. I'm waiting.

Jayden crept out from under the covers. He quietly got dressed and shoved his feet in his shoes, then curled his fingers around the doorknob to pull it open. He cringed when the hinges screamed. He managed to slip into the hall and through the hotel without waking anyone.

When he stepped out the side exit and onto the sidewalk, the warm, humid night air gave him a boost of energy. He searched in both directions, but the alley was empty and dark. "Hey," he called in a harsh whisper. "Where are you?"

Shut up. You're going to wake someone up. You don't have to talk, remember?

Jayden exhaled. Right. *Where are you?*

Across the street.

Jayden peered to the other side of the road and spotted a tiny silhouette under a street lamp. He jogged across the four deserted lanes to the other side, stopping in front of her. "Where to?"

She crossed her arms. *You still want to talk out loud. I don't get it.*

"Because it's normal, and I like to feel as normal as possible, if you don't mind."

She shrugged. "Fine. Have it your way. Come on." She pulled out a candy from her pocket and unwrapped it, then shoved it in her mouth. "So, you don't have to sleep, huh?" Her words were slurred as she chewed. "That's cool."

He shrugged. "Not really." Modem tossed the wrapper on the ground. "What are you eating?"

"Candy." She swallowed and pulled another one out of her pocket. "What? I'm not allowed to like candy anymore?"

He chuckled. "I didn't say that. I was just fishing for you to offer me one." He held out his hand. She put one in his palm and then unwrapped another and popped it in her mouth. "What about you?" he asked, peeling the yellow paper. His mouth watered. "Isn't it past your bedtime?"

She shot him a glare. "I don't really like to sleep."

"How is that even possible?" He slipped the candy between his lips, and lemon flavor burst over his tongue. "If I could sleep for a week straight, I would."

"Yeah, well…" She kicked at the sidewalk. The bounce in her step faded. "People like me don't always have the best dreams."

"People like you. You mean dreamwalkers?"

Modem's bushy ponytail bobbed with each step. "Is that what they call it?"

"I think so, if that's what you are." The pattering of distant footsteps over wet concrete caught his ear. He glanced over his shoulder at the empty sidewalk.

"So, what kind of pie do you like?" Modem asked, drawing back his attention.

"I don't know. What kind do they have?"

"My favorite is bean pie."

He crinkled his nose. "Gross."

"Don't knock it till you try it."

More steady footsteps made him stop. He turned, staring at the empty sidewalk and scoping both sides of the road, his eyes narrowing.

"What?" Modem whispered.

He shook his head. "Nothing," he said loud enough for anyone close enough to hear. "Just a cat or something." He grabbed Modem's wrist and yanked her into a side alley. Jayden pressed his index finger to his lips.

He held his breath, tuning in to every sound. Small trails of rainwater trickled from the gutters, tapping against the pavement. A TV blared from an apartment nearby. A few cars rolled past over the wet streets.

The faint rhythm returned.

Someone's following us, he thought.

Who?

With Contessa possibly aware he was onto her, it could have been anyone—or anything. He balled his fists. *Unless you can run really fast, don't let anyone see you.*

Modem nodded.

The steps grew louder. Jayden inched his way to the corner of the brick building, careful to stay shrouded in shadow. He couldn't steal a look until he was ready to be seen.

The footsteps stopped.

Jayden's gut twisted as he waited, listening.

There was just one chance to get this right. He had to take out whoever was following them on the first try. He may not get another.

A shadowed figure stepped into sight.

Jayden leaped out and swung.

His fist cracked the guy's nose, slapping the stranger to the pavement.

Light from a flickering streetlamp cast over the stalker's features. Blood trickled down his lips, dripping off his chin. He groaned. "I think you broke my nose."

Jayden's eyes widened. "Peter?"

The healer staggered to his feet, cradling his face with both hands. He spit blood onto the sidewalk. His eyes began to swell. "What was that for?"

"What did you expect? You snuck up on me. I

didn't…" Jayden stopped. "Wait. What the hell are you doing here?"

Peter spit another mouthful of blood. "I was sent here to find you. I thought the hotel was a good place to start looking. I figured Hawa might have taken you there. I've been scoping the place out for two days." He braced his fingers on both sides of his nose and snapped it back in place.

Jayden's stomach turned into a queasy cesspool of nausea. He swallowed the saliva pooled under his tongue. "You know about that place, huh?"

"Yeah." Peter wiped any remaining blood off his face with his t-shirt. "Hawa told me about it a few times. It took some serious searching to find it, though."

Which meant Peter knew some, but not all of what really went on there. That somehow made him feel special. He knew about Hawa's past when the others didn't, and that meant she trusted him.

"We haven't seen Zanya since the bonding ceremony," Peter continued, pulling Jay back to the moment. "She and Arwan took off right after. Zanya's mom completely lost it."

"Yeah." He shoved his hands in his pockets. "I remember."

"Zanya looked for you before she left. Her mom made a big deal about Arwan, and everyone at the bonding ceremony turned on him."

"It's hard to believe she even noticed I was gone." The swelling around Peter's eyes had already subsided. Luckily, he was a healer, and the broken nose would mend within the hour.

I'm assuming I don't have to run for my life?

Modem thought.

"Oh." He turned to the alleyway. "Sorry. You can come out."

She stepped out of the shadows, took one look at Peter's face, and sucked air between her teeth. "Ouch. That's gotta suck."

Peter examined the girl. "Who's this?"

Don't you dare tell him, Modem said. *Not who I really am.*

Jayden shrugged. "Just a kid from the hotel. I'm trying to keep her out of trouble."

Peter scoffed. "You're the last person qualified to do that."

"He's not so bad." She smiled at Peter. "I'm Modem." She extended her hand. Peter shook it. "Nice to meet you," she said. "So, you're friend of Jayden's?"

"Sometimes." He touched his nose, and his focus shifted back to Jay. "We need you back. Things have gotten bad. Really bad."

He analyzed the healer's stone features. This was serious. "What's going on?"

"It's Contessa. The witch has made some nasty friends, and she's summoning everything she's got. Soon, the middleworld will be overrun."

Modem sighed. "I guess that means no pie."

CHAPTER TWELVE

Soft hues of orange and red wavered in the sky as they approached the hotel. Modem yawned, her hands crossed over her chest and dark circles set under her eyes. All three of them walked toward the Thirteenth Street Hotel, turning their backs to the sun while it peeked over the crooked horizon.

Peter kept pace beside Jayden, the two of them walking in silence. It was good to see a familiar face, but couldn't it have been someone else? Anyone, as long as Hawa didn't used to be in love with him. The whole thing between her and Peter was over and gone, but she was still bitter. He could sense it. Every time she heard his name her shoulders tensed, and she could never look at the healer without a slight glare. She wouldn't take his help or offer any, and that was going to make things a lot more complicated.

"Listen." Jayden rubbed the back of his neck. "I don't know if it's a great idea Hawa knows you're here."

Peter nodded. "I was the only one she told about

the hotel before this. With you and Zanya gone, we couldn't seek Hawa. It was really our only option."

Even though Jay sensed her resentment, there was a lot about their relationship he didn't know. He recalled the day Peter was nearly killed by the beam in Renato's house after Sarian's attack. Jay's skin crawled every time the memory of Hawa's scream echoed through his mind. She'd been hysterical, like someone had lost the one person they loved. Funny how love could be bitter and sweet at the same time. His mind flashed to Zanya, and he blinked, willing away the memory. He still loved her, but something had shifted inside of him. Something that made him love her…differently.

"Why shouldn't she know I'm here?" Peter asked.

Jayden shrugged. "You know Hawa."

Peter huffed. "Yeah. I know."

Jayden stole a glance at the healer. "What else did she tell you about this place?"

"I don't know. Like what?"

"I mean, did she ever tell you about stuff that happened in the hotel, before Renato's?"

Peter shook his head. "Not really. She just said she grew up there, and it was a place for kids to go who had no home. Past that, she never really got into details." Peter looked over his shoulder at Modem. "I'm assuming there's a reason the girl is here—past trying to keep her out of trouble."

Jayden glanced back just in time to see her glare. *Don't do it.* He brushed his fingertips together, analyzing the situation. They had always been more powerful in numbers. *Peter is one of us,* he replied.

Jayden stopped walking and turned to Modem. "You know that, right? It's safe to tell him."

"Tell me what?" Peter paused. "What's going on?"

Modem stopped several feet away. She stared down the street, her eyes growing wider by the second.

Jayden's stomach dropped. He turned to find Hawa standing on the sidewalk with her hands on her hips, tapping her leather boot on the pavement.

"Shit." Jayden swallowed. "This isn't good."

Peter stepped back. "Maybe she doesn't recognize me."

Modem snorted. "She's mad. Not blind."

Hawa stomped toward them, meeting Peter toe-to-toe. Her full lips twisted into a snarl. "What are you doing here?"

"We're just hanging out, Brisa," Modem said. "Chill."

She cocked her head at the girl. "You should not be hanging out with these guys. Do you want Blade to flip out?"

"Why would he care, especially since you're together with him now?" She gestured to Jay. "Me hanging out with him shouldn't make a difference."

Peter's lips parted and his gaze ping-ponged between them. "Seriously?"

Hawa's glare snapped back to Peter. "That is *none* of your business." She stepped back, examining all three of them. Hawa crossed her arms, tapping her fingers on her biceps. "Who's first?"

Jayden pointed at Peter. "He came here looking

for me."

Modem rolled her eyes. "Narc."

"Why?" Hawa demanded.

"Because we need his help," Peter added. "We could use yours too."

"Not happening." She grabbed Jayden's hand. "Come on. Time to go."

"Go?" Modem said. "Where?"

"Away." Hawa wove her fingers together with Jayden's. "You were right. We should just get out of here." She glared over her shoulder at Peter. "Apparently I can't have any privacy, no matter how far I go."

"But…" Modem's voice had become more distant. "I want to come."

Hawa turned to face the girl. "Sorry, Modem, but you can't come with us."

"So you're just going to leave again, like you did last time?" The kid's eyes glossed with tears. Suddenly Jayden couldn't see the powerful dreamwalker under the desperate little girl in front of them. "You can't…you can't just leave me here."

Hawa glanced at Jay, then sighed. She let go of his hand and walked toward her. "Listen." Her voice had lost its razor edge, and she crouched in front of Modem. "Sometimes we have to do things we don't really want to." Hawa touched her arm. "I can't stay here anymore. One day you'll understand."

Modem's throat visibly tightened, and she stepped back. "You never really cared about us, did you? It was all about Blade. It was always about him."

"That's not true, Modem. I care—"

"No!" Her normally steady voice cracked. "If you cared, you wouldn't leave again."

Hawa stood. "I'm sorry you're angry. Maybe you're just too young to understand."

Modem shook her head. Her hands curled into fists and her body began to shake.

"Um…" Jayden stepped back. "Maybe we should…take cover…"

Hawa arched an eyebrow. "She's a kid, not a wrecking ball."

Modem's eyes inked into pools of black.

"Don't be so sure." He quickly inspected the buildings around them, searching for a shield of brick or metal.

The air stilled and all sounds drifted into complete silence.

"Seriously. We need to get out of here." He took Hawa's hand. The ground below them began to shake. Pebbles bounced on the paved sidewalk. The light from the streetlamp overhead shattered, sparking as shards of glass rained over them.

Hawa covered her head and ducked out of the way. "What's happening?"

"She's upset," Jayden said. "I think she's still learning how to control her powers."

Hawa dropped her hands to her sides, gawking at him. *"Powers?"*

The rusted iron balconies attached to the apartment buildings overhead shuddered and creaked. Brick dust coated the sidewalk in a thin layer of red. A random person on the sidewalk a few blocks down screamed and ran, shouting,

"Terremoto!"

"They think it's an earthquake," Hawa shouted. The light post began to buckle, the metal screaming under the pressure of Modem's powers.

Jayden looked at the kid. *You have to stop. You're going to hurt someone.*

Ear-piercing shrieks clawed at his mind. He cupped his hands over his ears and clenched his eyes shut.

Hawa grabbed Jayden and yanked him into a narrow alley just as the light post snapped and crashed onto the sidewalk. After a moment, things quieted.

When he opened his eyes, Hawa's glare was fierce.

"It wasn't my fault," he blurted.

"Ugh." She shoved him back and stepped onto the main sidewalk. When her gaze found Modem, she pressed her fingers over her lips. "Oh my God."

Jayden stepped out, following Hawa as she ran to Modem's frail frame crumpled to the pavement. She held her hands over the kid's body. "Peter! Where the hell are you?"

The healer inched out of a nook where he'd found shelter, and looked in their direction.

"Get over here," Hawa shouted. "She needs help!"

Peter jogged to them and knelt beside Modem. He rested his hands on her shoulders and closed his eyes.

Jayden shifted. "Is she okay?" He held his breath, waiting for the answer.

"Shh." Peter drew in a deep breath. After a

stretched moment of silence, he finally opened his eyes. "She's exhausted."

"That's it?" Hawa said.

"I mean, she's not physically hurt, but her abilities are all over the place."

Hawa buried her fingers in her hair. "How couldn't I see this sooner?"

"Because she didn't want you to," Jayden said.

Peter shot her an annoyed glare. "I can see why."

"What the hell is that supposed to mean?" she snapped.

Peter ignored her question. "This kid packs a serious punch. If she wanted, she could do a lot of damage."

Hawa examined the snapped light post and shattered glass, the crumbled cement and brick dust blanketing the sidewalk. "She did this?"

"She's got this thing…" Jayden scratched his head. "Like, when she gets pissed, she kind of loses it."

Hawa looked at him. "You knew and didn't tell me?"

"I just found out, and she made me swear not to say anything." Kind of the truth.

"And you listened to her? She's a kid, for God's sake!"

"She's one of us." Jayden pressed his lips into a tight line. "She needs help. She needs someone to teach her how to use her powers before she kills someone."

"Or herself." Peter pushed to his feet. "We need to get her out of here."

Jayden had nearly forgotten they were standing

in the open, in the middle of Guatemala City. He crouched down and scooped Modem into his arms. Her cheeks were pale, and her limp body hung lifeless. If she weren't breathing, he'd think she was gone.

"Let's get her back to the hotel before anyone starts asking questions." Hawa glared at Peter. "You. Go home."

Peter shook his head. "I can't. Not without you guys."

"I'll come back when I'm good and ready. Not when *you* tell me to." She turned to Jayden. "Let's go. Now."

When Jayden turned to follow, Peter grabbed his arm. "Listen to me. I wouldn't have come down here if it weren't our last resort. We need you back. We need your ability to find Zanya, and I don't have time for Hawa's power struggles."

Jayden frowned. "I wish I could help. I really do, but…" He exhaled. "I have to stay with Hawa. She needs me more than you do right now."

"So that's it?" Peter stepped back. "Now that Zanya's gone, you're okay with ditching everyone?"

"Ditching everyone?" he squared his stance with Peter's. "Nobody wants me there unless they can use me for something. I sacrificed *years* in that orphanage with Zanya. I followed her to Renato's house in the middle of butt-fuck nowhere to help. Renato doesn't want me there, Marzena doesn't want me there, and Zanya can take care of herself." Jayden took a step back. "Besides." His throat tightened. "She has Arwan now. They're together, and he won't let anything happen to her."

"Arwan can't protect her from what's coming. Nobody can."

Jayden shifted his weight. "Zanya's the Guardian. She'll—"

"No." Peter squared his jaw. "She won't. She left, and without working together, we're all as good as dead." His gaze flickered down the street. "Including Hawa. And she'll never know it's coming."

Jayden glanced over his shoulder at Hawa, who was nearing the end of the block. Even if it killed him to admit it, the healer was right. If things had really gotten that bad, without working together, everyone would go down. He exhaled. "Just give me a little time. She'll never agree if she feels forced." He looked down at Modem. "And Modem needs time to rest." He turned his back to Peter and jogged to catch up to Hawa.

When the girl woke up, Hawa would have a serious tongue lashing to deal out. Then they could move on. Work together. If Peter was right...if Contessa was really that close to raising the underworld, they had to act as a team, and they had to move fast.

First, he'd have to convince Hawa to come along.

Chapter Thirteen

Hawa paced the room of the Thirteenth Street Hotel while Modem sat on the mattress, sipping a soda. Peter wasn't allowed in, at risk of being seen by Blade and causing a bloodbath.

Jayden stood beside the window, his hands tucked in his front pockets. "You're going to wear out the carpet."

"Shut up. This is your fault."

"It's my fault Modem's a dreamwalker?"

"It's your fault she had an episode on the sidewalk, and we don't know she's a dreamwalker for sure." She mumbled a few sentences in Spanish, spinning the silver ring around her finger.

Modem set the empty can of soda on the floor. "You don't have to worry about me." Her voice had been hoarse since she came to. "I don't need anything from you. I don't want you to treat me any different."

"But you are different." Hawa stopped pacing and gazed down at her. "You're like us. Different. You'll have to get used to that if you don't want your power to control you for the rest of your life."

Modem's tiny features turned to stone. "This is exactly why I didn't want to tell you."

"I could have helped you."

"Like you are now?"

Hawa's lips parted.

"How about both of you calm down for a minute," Jayden interrupted. "This could be a good thing."

Modem pushed to her feet. Her legs wobbled beneath her and she leaned on the wall to catch her breath. "This whole thing is so messed up. You were never supposed to find out."

"But now that she knows, we can do this together," Jayden said.

"What the hell are you talking about?" Hawa snapped.

Jayden glanced at her. "They need us."

Hawa's eyes darkened. "You want to go after Contessa?"

"Peter said—"

"Are you shitting me?" Hawa groaned and rubbed her temples. "You want to help him?"

"No." Jayden pushed off the wall and stepped into the middle of the room. "I want *us* to do it. You, me, and the kid."

Modem rolled her eyes, probably too weak to scold him for calling her a kid.

"Why do you even care?" Hawa said. "You left. Checked out. Why get involved?"

"Because Renato and his band of groupies can't beat this on their own. I thought they could. I didn't think Zanya would actually leave, but that's not how it played out. Without Zanya, I'm the only one who can seek Contessa and steal the book." Jayden shifted his weight. "If we don't help, everything will suffer. Not just Renato and everyone in his precious mansion, but the hotel, too. It will all crumble, along with the rest of the middleworld when the demons rise. We won't stand a chance." He looked at Modem. "None of us will."

Hawa's shoulders relaxed. "Oh." She stood up straight and grinned. "Why didn't you just say so?"

Jayden threw his hands in the air. "Unbelievable. That's all it took?"

Hawa shrugged. "I can't be the reason these kids..." She blinked and swallowed. "I care about them."

Modem sucked in a labored breath. "I don't know if I can..." Sweat collected on her brow, streaking down her face. Her legs buckled and she fell to the floor. Her eyes fluttered shut.

Jayden scooped her up and laid her back onto the mattress, then gently pulled the covers over her. "It's too soon. She needs more time."

"Then we make a plan, and when she's ready, we go in."

"Go in, where?"

Hawa's grin widened. "The underworld."

Even though it wasn't possible, it was still pretty badass she was willing to risk everything. Jayden took her hand and pulled her into him. "I knew there was a reason I..."

She cocked her head. "You what?"

He wanted to say he liked her, but it was more than that.

Her smile blossomed. "I didn't know it was like that."

He grinned. So much for keeping his thoughts to himself.

Hawa pressed a kiss on his lips, and he curled his fingers around a handful of her hair, sliding his tongue over hers. When she shifted closer, her body felt like home.

She pulled away and gazed at Modem, now asleep. "I can't believe it. She's like us. Everything changed so fast."

"Yeah." That was the understatement of the century. "You think she'll be okay? I mean, after she learns more about her ability?"

Hawa tucked a few strands of hair behind her ear, adorned in rows of silver earrings. "I don't know. Being a dreamwalker isn't something I'd want for anyone. Being trapped forever in a kid's body? It's like a bad dream."

Jayden frowned. "When we tell her, I hope she can deal with it. Without hurting herself, I mean."

Hawa exhaled. "Yeah. Do you think she'd be better off with Renato? She wouldn't be the first Riyata he helped ease into their place in the world." She met his gaze. "I don't think I can do it. I don't think I can take care of her like she needs."

"We'll figure it out." He held her close and pressed his cheek against hers. "As far as going to the underworld, we can't." When Zanya had returned from retrieving his soul from the underworld, she'd told him all about the cave and the portal, and how Arwan had offered his half-underworld blood as a sacrifice for entrance.

Without that, they'd never get through. And unfortunately for him, even though he'd spent some time in the underworld, he didn't bleed. Not anymore.

"Contessa won't come to the middleworld again until she has a solid plan. Last time she was here, she was falling apart at the seams, remember? She's in the underworld because she's fading, and there she can feed off the damned souls. We have to assume the worst."

There was a slight knock on the door. Hawa slipped out of Jayden's arms and opened the hotel room door.

"Hey, Brisa." The little boy they called Tic-Tac stood at the door.

"Hey, buddy." She opened the door wider. "What's going on?"

"Um…" He twisted the fabric of his shirt in his tiny hands.

Hawa glanced at Jay, then back to the kid. "What is it?"

Tic-Tac gestured to the foyer with a nod of his head. "Blade wants you. He sent me up. Said it's important and to meet him down there…now."

Hawa nodded. "Okay. Thanks. I'll be down in a minute." She ruffled his hair.

"I don't think he'll wait a minute." Fear streaked his tone, clearly setting Hawa on high alert.

She crouched in front of him. "What's wrong?" She rested her hand on his shoulder.

Tic-Tac flinched away.

Hawa gently pulled down the neckline of his shirt to expose a yellow and blue bruise on the boy's collarbone. She winced. "What happened?"

Tic-Tac lowered his head. "I'm fine."

"Did Blade do this to you?"

Tic-Tac responded with a sniffle.

Hawa pushed to her feet, her hands balled into tight fists. "Why don't you stay here with Modem?" she said in a low growl. Hawa guided the boy inside. "I'm sure she'll be happy to see you when she wakes up."

Tic-Tac nodded. "Okay." He sniffled and wiped his nose with the back of his hand. "Sure."

Jayden looked down at Tic-Tac and winked. "You're one tough little dude."

"Blade says I have to be. He says life is too hard for me to be weak."

Jayden's features sobered. "He said that, huh?"

Tic-Tac nodded.

Jayden examined the boy's bright eyes. He was too innocent to be here, in this place, without parents or a family to take care of him. His chest tightened. "Promise me something." The boy stared up at him, waiting. "If you hear people shouting or things breaking downstairs, don't come out, okay?" The boy paused, swallowed, and nodded. "Good." He pointed at Modem. "Keep an eye on her for me. I'm counting on you." He reached out to pat the kid on his back, but pulled back his hand, afraid he might hurt him if there were any more bruises they couldn't see.

Hawa had already left the room and was halfway down the stairs by the time Jay caught up.

She walked with a purpose, her focus trained on Blade.

Jay slowed when they reached the bottom floor. He circled around the room, recalling what Modem had said about making things worse.

"*Hijo de puta!*" Hawa swung a right hook and landed it square on Blade's jaw.

Jayden raised his eyebrows. So much for not making things worse.

Blade stumbled, and the back of his legs buckled over the fountain in the center of the foyer. She shook her hand, sucking in a sharp breath through her teeth.

Blade wiped a streak of blood from the corner of his mouth. "Are you flirting with me, Brisa?"

She scowled. "I'll show you flirting." She charged him.

Blade stood, his eyes dark, grinning a sinister smile. "Here we go," he said under his breath, almost too low for Jayden to hear.

Hawa swung again. Blade blocked the assault and punched her in the gut.

Hawa gasped and collapsed to the floor, clawing at the aged wood as she gulped in shallow breaths.

Jayden stepped forward. Hawa extended her hand, coughing through labored breaths. "Stay out of this," she croaked.

The hotel became eerily silent. Jayden looked up as the hotel room doors quietly clicked shut, everyone vanishing from sight. It was like they had seen this a thousand times, and knew it would get ugly.

Jayden returned his focus to Blade. His gut twisted, fury boiling in his veins. He'd kill that piece of shit. He'd kill him, and wouldn't lose a moment of sleep over it.

Hawa stumbled to her feet, forcing herself to stand on her own.

Blade chuckled. "You sure you want to go for round two, *Brisa*? You know what you're getting yourself into. You should remember well enough."

She drew in deep breaths, her glare deepening. "*You* should remember," she wheezed. "I'm used to it." With her lips pursed into a tight, rigid line, she leaped forward and swung her elbow, cracking Blade in the mouth.

He backhanded her across the cheek, sending her spinning. She stayed on her feet and squared her shoulders, her fists in the air.

Jayden shifted as jolts of electricity bolted through his muscles. He couldn't just stand there and watch Blade beat her black and blue. Hawa's cheek had already begun to swell. An ugly purple shadow blotted the fair skin under her eye.

Her gaze flickered to Jayden for just a second. She shook her head, and clenched her fists. "You have no right to hurt these kids, Blade."

He strutted toward her, his hands at his sides, making no effort to guard himself. Hawa tightened her jaw. Knowing her, it was clear *that* insulted Hawa even more than Blade's smug laugh.

"No right?" Blade echoed. He scowled. "You, of all people, have no room to talk about rights." Blade pushed out his chest. His gaze dragged down Hawa's body to her belly, where his gaze lingered for a long moment. "You don't give a damn about rights."

"Go to hell," Hawa growled. "You know it

wasn't my choice."

"Oh, really? So you didn't call me from the clinic? I'm just…" He shrugged. "Imagining it all?"

"So stupid," she mumbled. "I was so stupid to call you. I should have never—" Her voice caught in her throat. Her fists slightly relaxed, and her gaze drifted. "I can still hear her heartbeat…" A tear slipped down her cheek.

Jayden's chest hollowed with a silent exhale.

Modem never did tell him how far along she was when she lost the baby. She could have had plenty of doctor appointments before it happened.

"You," Blade said, stealing Jayden's attention. "You never wanted her."

Hawa shook her head. "That's not true."

"You got rid of her," he continued in a deep, ominous tone.

"No." Hawa swallowed. "I knew I couldn't take care of her. She would have ended up in this hotel, like these kids."

"Bullshit." Blade glared at her stomach. "You tore her out of you."

"No!" Hawa's shriek echoed through the empty foyer. "You stole her from me. You hurt her. You *killed* her!"

Hawa sprinted forward and collided with Blade. They both went down in a ball of flying fists. Blade grabbed Hawa by the shoulders and rolled on top of her, then coiled his fingers around her neck, bearing down with all of his weight.

Hawa's eyes widened, and she kicked under him, clawing at Blade's wrists.

Jayden tore Blade off and grabbed him by his

shirt, lifting him to his feet. He drew Blade's face an inch from his. "That's the last time you'll ever touch her."

Blade grabbed his arms, digging his fingers into Jay's muscles. "Then I won't be the only one." Blade shoved Jay back and threw a right hook, cracking his solid knuckle against Jay's cheekbone.

Jay stumbled back and blinked repeatedly, shaking off the rattled daze. He curled his lips into a grin. "That all you got?" Jayden ran forward and tackled him like a cornerback, slamming Blade into the wall.

Blade snatched the knife from his side and pressed it to Jay's throat. "If I take off your head, will you die then?"

Jayden jumped back. Good question. *Something* had to kill him, and decapitation seemed like a pretty sure way to get it done.

Blade raised the knife and lunged forward, bringing it down at Jayden's chest. Jay spun and punched Blade in the back of his head, sending his face slamming into the floor. When Blade turned on his back, blood drizzled from his mouth, down his chin.

Hawa ran between them, extending her hands.

Jayden froze.

"It doesn't have to be like this."

Jayden examined her hunched posture and the circular bruise encompassing her neck. "How's it going to be, then? Blade beating up on you some more, and you running to save him?"

She stood up a bit straighter. "No. But you don't have to be like him. You're better than that."

Jayden ground his teeth. "Maybe." He shifted, the heat in his gut slowly cooling. "I want to be."

Hawa smiled softly. "I know it."

Blade stood, and Jayden caught the motion over Hawa's shoulder. Her ex loomed behind her, his eye twitching, and he lifted the knife to his side, aiming the pointed steel at her back.

Jayden sucked in a sharp breath. "Move!"

Hawa dropped on instinct, just as Blade jabbed the glistening weapon in the air. Jayden seized Blade's wrist as tightly as he could and gave it a swift twist. The loud snap of bone made even him wince.

Blade shouted, and the knife clattered to the floor.

Jay grabbed the fabric of Blade's shirt and punched him in the face once, twice, three times—after a few moments he'd lost count. But Blade's inner fight was stronger than Jay had anticipated. Even with blood dribbling down Blade's nose and his lip split open, he managed to land a solid punch to Jay's gut, tearing open the stitches from the knife wound Hawa had stitched.

Jay stumbled up the stairs as Blade pushed forward, raw fury burning in his contorted features. Blade swung again, missing his target. It didn't take long for him to charge forward, forcing Jay further up the stairs to the upper floor.

Swaying at the top of the stairs, Blade gave a bloody, sinister smile. "She may not want me, but if I can't have her, neither can you." He charged forward and plowed into Jayden like a pissed off bull seeing red. Blade crashed through rusted iron, taking Jayden down with him. They fell three stories, and the wood boards cracked and splintered when they hit the floor.

CHAPTER FOURTEEN

Jayden blinked open his eyes, fog drifting around the edge of his vision. With a grunt, he rolled off Blade and onto the cool, wood floor.

"Jayden." Hawa's voice was breathless. He lifted his head and found her, hunched on the floor, clutching her stomach with one hand while the other pressed over her lips. She slowly stood. "What have you done?"

"What?" He blinked again, still trying to recall what had happened that day. Everything was cloudy and muddled.

Hawa shook her head, staring at the person beside him.

Jayden scowled, planted his hands on the floor, and pushed himself up. His fingers landed in something thick, wet, and warm. When he picked up his hand, scarlet covered his fingertips, dripping down his palm. "What…"

Run. Modem's voice brought it all rushing back.

Jayden sprang to his feet, still staring at his blood-coated hand. He looked at Hawa, whose gaze was now locked on him, and not Blade's lifeless body.

"We need to get out of here," Jayden said softly. He quickly analyzed himself by tightening his muscles, surprised he didn't take any damage from the fall. He swallowed against a dry throat and fisted his hands. "Now."

The creaking of rusty hinges on hotel room doors filled the air. He raised his gaze to a few of the orphan kids who were now in the hall, some of them leaning over the railing, staring down at the scene below.

I said run, while you still can. Modem's voice in his head somehow soothed the sheer panic streaking through him.

I can't just leave you here, Jayden replied.

Tiny whispers from the orphan kids carried through the air, growing louder by the second.

I'm not strong enough to walk.

He turned to Hawa. "I'm getting Modem, and we're getting out of here."

Hawa nodded. "We better hurry." She approached Blade's body and crouched beside him. After a moment of hesitation, she glided her hand over his face, closing his eyes. "I'm sorry." A tear slid down her cheek, but this time she didn't wipe it. "I wish things could have been different."

Jayden tried not to watch, but he couldn't look away.

Hawa sniffled and reached into Blade's front pocket, pulling out an old flip phone. She opened it and pressed a few buttons, then held it to her ear.

She must have been calling Peter. That was the

smart thing to do right now. They would need him.

Jayden left Hawa to the call and dashed up the stairs, trying to ignore the wide eyes and tiny faces of the children he passed in the halls. Some were crying. Others were pale and standing with their backs pressed against the wall, dirt streaked over their faces. One tiny girl was curled into a ball, rocking herself back and forth in the doorway. He paused beside her, but couldn't find the courage to speak.

After a few more strides, he flung open the door to the room Modem and Tic-Tac were in. Modem stood with Tic-Tac's support. Her arm was slung around his shoulder, both of them making their way toward the hall.

Jayden ruffled Tic-Tac's hair and winked. "You did good, kid." He scooped Modem in his arms and gestured toward the hall with a nod. "Let's go."

"Me too?" Tic-Tac said, blinking up at him.

"Hell yeah, you too."

Tic-Tac beamed. "Yes!"

As he darted out the door, Jayden snagged him by the arm and swung him around. "Listen to me." He crouched as low as he could with Modem in his arms. "When you go out there, don't look over the railing. Don't look around at all, even when you get down to the foyer, you got it? Just keep your eyes down, and go from this door, to that main exit." He jabbed his finger in the air as he spoke.

"O…okay." Tic-Tac nodded.

"Good." He stood and waved him on. "Run."

Jayden cradled Modem tighter against his chest and gazed down at her pale cheeks and limp, curly hair hanging around her face. "You up for this?"

"I kind of have to be, don't I?" Her voice quivered, but it was stronger than before.

"Yeah, I guess you do." Jayden drew in a deep breath and walked forward, through the hall, down the stairs, and to Hawa's side.

Modem nestled her face against Jayden's chest. Her small fingers curled around his shirt. *Is it bad?*

Thick blood had pooled under Blade's body, reaching out in tiny rivers, flowing into the seams of the beaten hardwood floor. Jayden clenched his jaw. *Yeah, it's bad.*

All he'd wanted to do was take Blade out. Now that Blade was dead, he'd give anything to take it back. Blade may have been the world's biggest douche bag, and maybe even a killer, but he'd kept all these kids alive, and Jay had stripped them of that protection—however little it may have been.

Tic-Tac's tiny footsteps grew louder behind him until the kid passed them to the front door. He walked straight out, onto the sidewalk without a word.

"Where's Peter?" Jayden asked. Modem was weak, and could use a healing session.

Hawa shrugged. "I haven't talked to him." She wiped the cellphone clean with her sleeve and then tossed it beside Blade's body.

Sirens pierced the air.

Jayden stared at the phone, then dragged his gaze back to Hawa. "What did you do?"

Hawa looked up at the dozens of hotel room doors and the hallways with kids staring down at them. "It's over. These kids need a real home."

Jayden's throat tightened as his focus shifted, and he watched Tic-Tac standing outside the open door. "What about the kid?"

Hawa stole a glance over her shoulder. "He needs a good home more than anyone."

"So he's not coming," he said, more as a statement than a question. Her silence gave him the answer he needed. The sirens grew louder. "Are we going to tell him?"

"We don't have any time. The police will be here soon, and if we don't want to end up in handcuffs, we have to go."

She was right. He knew she was right. It was the right thing to do. Even so, it was still seriously fucked up.

There's no time. Modem's voice snapped him out of his thoughts.

Jayden took one last, long look at Tic-Tac through the smudgy glass doors. With a good home, he'd have a chance to grow up and be someone. He deserved that much. He turned and carried Modem to the side exit, Hawa hot on his heels.

***

Jayden watched Peter open the windows in the Marriott suite he'd reserved for a few days. "I talked to Renato. He was happy to hear everyone's okay." A warm breeze swept through the room, whipping around the sheer curtains and playing with strands of Hawa's dark hair.

Hawa sat on the king size bed at Modem's feet, her hand rested on the kid's foot. "Did you tell

Renato about her?"

Peter nodded. "He was just as surprised as the rest of us. He said he hasn't seen another dreamwalker in decades."

Jayden leaned against the wall, his arms crossed and his gaze trained on Modem. "How much longer before she's good to travel?"

Peter crossed the room pressed his hand over Modem's forehead. "She's getting better. There's color back in her cheeks. I don't sense the fatigue like before, so she should be waking up soon."

"What about her ability?" Jayden asked. "Is it still freaking out?"

"Not that I can tell," Peter said.

"Good." Hawa stood. "When she's better, we can bring her down to the police station and—"

"What?" Jayden pushed off the wall. "What are you talking about? She's coming with us."

"No, she's not."

"Yes, *she is.*" Jayden narrowed his eyes. "We can't throw her into the system. Especially in Guatemala. No telling what foster care is like here."

"I know it's hard, but she'll be better off."

"Listen to me." He stepped toward Hawa and took her hand. "I grew up in the system, remember? I know what it's like. As soon as whatever case worker is assigned to her realizes she's different, they're going to throw her in the kind of place me and Zanya grew up in." He tightened his jaw. "I wouldn't wish that on anyone."

"And coming to Renato's with us will mean she's always looking over her shoulder. If you haven't realized, shit is about to hit the fan.

Contessa is getting stronger, and we don't know if we'll be able to fight her off when the time comes. Bringing Modem along will just put her in more danger."

Peter rested his hands on both of their shoulders. "Why don't you guys let her decide for herself?"

Jayden turned and looked at the girl, her big brown eyes blinking open. She parted her lips and drew in a deep breath, then stretched her arms over her head, as if she'd just woken up from the world's best nap. "Hey guys…" She pushed up onto her forearms, skimming over the faces in the room. "What's…what's going on?" She looked around the suite. "Whoa. Where are we?" A faint smile touched her lips as she ran her hands over the plush comforter adorned with satin threads.

Hawa gathered Modem's coat and shoes from the corner of the room and placed them on the bed. "Get dressed. We have to get moving."

"Moving, where?" Modem sat up straight and retied her dark, curled hair back into a puffy bun.

Hawa studied Jayden's rigid shoulders and tightly pursed lips.

If she cared about him past the convenient fling, she wouldn't make him leave Modem to the fucked up fate she was in for.

"Brisa?" Modem's tiny voice carried through the air with the warm wind. "Where are we going?"

Hawa studied him a moment longer, and let out a long, soft exhale. "To Renato's." She displayed a warm smile. "Where else?"

Jayden grinned. He'd never wanted to kiss her so much in his life. Doing it now would just be…weird, so he took her hand instead, and squeezed it extra tight. "Let's get our stuff together and—" A sharp, piercing pain tore through his temples, shrouding his vision in black, forcing him to his knees. He gripped his hair and ground his teeth before a scream tore out of his chest.

A pair of hands rested on his shoulders, but he couldn't define who it was. Then another. His muscles coiled and he curled into a ball, pressing his forehead harder against the floor as the moment stretched, and the pain bore deeper into his mind.

CHAPTER FIFTEEN

Flashes of light blinded him as the pain lifted, leaving him standing in a fog. He shifted his feet in cool sand, and craned his neck to see the seemingly dormant roots of the underworld overhead. A chill ran over his skin.

He turned, squinting through thick fog. He could barely see a few feet in front of him, let alone far enough to figure out what the hell was going on. And why was the underworld so cold? Assuming he was in the underworld…

"Hello?" Calling out probably wasn't the best idea, but he had little choice. If he stumbled around this realm, he could land in some pretty bad shit. "Um…" He stepped forward carefully, feeling each patch of sand beneath his feet before taking his next step. "Hello?"

"I have been expecting you," a voice purred from the blanket of fog.

Jayden spun and peered through the clouds, his heart bursting into overdrive. That voice. That silken, alluring voice. It could only be one person.

A moment later, a shadow appeared in the distance revealing curves like a goddess and long, thin limbs.

A knot tightened in his gut. "Why do I keep seeking you?" He shifted back as the shadow grew closer, and bits of Contessa's features became clear. The fog swirled and snaked around her as she pushed through it with every step.

"Perhaps your heart is tied to this realm. After all, your soul is tainted from this place. Perhaps your spirit yearns to return home." She stepped closer—close enough for her bright green eyes and polished, pink lips to tempt him.

Jayden shifted back again, recalling Renato's warning about the witch. She was beautiful, but that was her poison. She would consume his soul if she seduced him…if he still had a soul anymore, like she claimed.

"Perhaps your heart is tied to *me*." She tilted her head, displaying her long, elegant neck, and the sharp angle of her jaw line, half-hidden beneath waves of red, glistening hair. "You have been watching me. I've felt you close." She curled one side of her mouth into a tempting smile and leaned into him, her lips inches from his. "What is it that you want, *boy*?"

Jayden's breaths were sharp and shallow, uneasy from Contessa's hot breath caressing his mouth. He swallowed, staring at her lips. His muscles coiled as he fought an unbearable urge to dive into her entirely.

"Our souls are aligned, you know. We are like each other, you and I. Both from this realm. Both with—" She bit her bottom lip. "Desires." Contessa rested her hands on his chest.

Jayden winced beneath her touch. He swallowed and forced himself to speak. "What happened here?"

"This realm is under new rule. The king and I. Well…" She licked her lips. "We came to an arrangement." His skin flushed with a sick heat where she had rested her hands. The warmth reached into his muscles, asking him to move in closer. Caught in a bewitched haze, Jayden reached up and brushed his thumb across her cheek. Her skin was like milk, flawless and glowing. She turned her head and brushed her lips across his palm, spiking his blood with adrenaline. "Be wary." Her voice was softer this time. "You may find more than you can bear."

Jayden's skin was like fire. He sucked in a breath and blinked away the trance luring him into her. Jayden dropped his hands. "What do you want from me?"

She laughed again, but this time with a sharper edge. Her eyes narrowed. "You unfortunate boy. You never did stand a chance, did you?"

"What are you talking about?" He had to get out of there, fast. Without Modem to keep him safe, he'd have to help himself. Reclaim his ability, control it, and somehow find an escape.

"Death, followed by a brief resurrection," she continued. "The love of your life rejects you, and then bonds with another. You flee, and find comfort in another woman's arms. Now…" She sighed, curling her fingers around his shirt. "Now you find yourself here, again, in this realm." She clutched his shirt tighter. "Which you will not again escape."

Jayden's hands shook as Contessa's sickness brushed against his heart.

She clenched her jaw. "I will not allow you to sabotage my new empire." Contessa's eyes rolled with dark magic, shadows slithering under her once-fair skin. "Aside from the Guardian, you are the only Riyata left with the ability to seek. Yet you are the only Riyata who can seek with open access to my new realm, *underworlder*."

"What?" Jayden swayed and grasped Contessa's forearm, his legs losing strength. What was she talking about? He wasn't an underworlder. He wasn't like her. "What do you mean?" His voice faded into a mere exhale as the witch's icy power coiled around his heart.

"It is in fact a rare privilege, seeker, to have underworld ties. How very unfortunate you will not live to understand your true potential."

Panic spiked through his mind and he fell to the ground, scrambling away, his fingers raking through the sand. His mouth gaped as he tried to pull in a breath, but it was if the air had turned to stone. An invisible vise had clamped down on his lungs. His eyes widened as fog clouded his mind, and his heart became like a molten rock, sucking the life out of him with every passing moment.

The air around him shook, and a wavering wall of water plowed between them, spitting sand in every direction.

"Can you be any dumber?" Modem said from beside him.

The familiar wall of water shot up in front of

him. Jayden gasped in a breath, desperately clawing at the ground.

As the sick heat lifted from his chest, he drew in several more breaths. "I didn't do this," he choked out, struggling to rise to his hands and knees. His muscles quivered.

"That doesn't matter now." Modem swayed while she stood beside him. "I can't hold the barrier for long."

Jayden forced himself to his feet and turned to face Contessa. Modem's protective wall had not only severed Contessa's hold on him, but now shielded them from all directions. The temptress stood on the other side of the rippling barrier, staring at the wall with a slight tilt of her head. Her eyes flashed with a glint of darkness, and her lips parted. "Fascinating." She stepped toward the barrier. "This is what withheld your presence. I was sure I had sensed someone nearby." She reached out and touched the barrier, making it shudder. Tiny veins of black crawled over the spot she had touched.

Modem groaned and clutched her stomach. "Whoa." She blinked and tightened her grip on her belly. "Just her touch hurts. She's no small fish, is she?"

Jayden shook his head. "No, she's not." He examined Modem's contorted features. For a kid, she was putting up with a whole hell of a lot of pain. "How much does it hurt?" He reached out to her.

She held out her hand with a flat palm. "Don't." Her throat tightened. "I'm barely holding it together as it is. We need to get out of here."

Jayden paused, searching his mind for a way out. "You." He gestured toward the barrier. "I usually came back after the wall of water hit me. Not always, but it's worth a try. You need to get us out of here, not me."

"I guess it's the only chance we've got." She stood up a little straighter. "You ready?"

Jayden nodded. "Does a bear shi—" He snapped his jaw shut. "Um, yeah. Totally ready."

Modem let her hands fall to her sides and curled her fingers into fists. She drew in a deep breath and exhaled. Her chest dropped, and her features softened.

Jayden waited for ice-cold water to crash into him, but the barrier hadn't moved. Contessa walked along the wavering wall, skimming her fingers along it, leaving streaks of black in her wake.

Modem opened her eyes and looked around. "Something's wrong."

"What?"

"I…" Modem shifted. "I tried, and it didn't work. She must be manipulating my mind somehow."

Particulates of soil fell from above them, landing on the barrier shielding them. He snapped his head up to see roots from the tree shift and churn in the sky as if it were waking up from hibernation.

"Even if I did allow you leave this realm a second time," Contessa said, "you are too late." She extended her hand above her head, as if reaching out to the tree. "And after you are gone, there will be no other with the ability to seek, and who also holds ties to the underworld. No other to observe me in times of necessary discretion."

Modem gawked at the tree above them, her cheeks drained of color, and her eyes growing wider by the second. "*Oh my God...*"

Jayden scanned the abandoned realm, spotting the distant shadow of a ruin within run-like-hell distance. Jayden glanced up at the tree's roots again, only to see them reaching down from the soil. "Go!" Jayden dashed toward her. Modem stood, her neck craned and mouth gaping. She'd been in the underworld before, but always behind her own barrier. Now it was a world torn wide open, ready to swallow her whole. "I said run, damn it! Go!"

A booming crash echoed in his ears. He stole a glance over his shoulder just as a second root from the tree crashed through Modem's barrier, punching a hole in the shield.

Modem's feet were stuck fast to the ground while she continued to stare up at the tree. She might have been in shock, but there was no time to explain what was happening. If they didn't find cover soon, they wouldn't have a second chance to escape. He scooped her into his arms as he passed and ran faster than he'd thought possible. A third root slammed through the barrier. Black shadows spread through the wall in thick veins, as if the tree had poisoned it with its assaults.

With every frantic step, the stone ruin grew closer. Jayden slipped on the sand, and quickly gained traction again, just in time to dive behind the base of ruin. Panting, he pressed his back against the cold stone, searching for his next grand idea.

Now they were stuck, with nowhere to go and nothing but a pissed off woman and a man-eating tree trying to turn them both into an evening snack.

"Damn it, damn it, damn it." He pressed his head harder against the stone, pressing his eyes shut. "I don't know what to do." He turned to Modem. "Any ideas?"

From the sudden awareness behind her eyes, she'd snapped out of her daze. She shook her head. Dreamwalker or not, she was still just a kid, and he was the only one around to protect her.

"Okay." He nodded, hoping for a miracle. That'd happened once already when Zanya broke him out of the underworld. It wasn't likely to happen again.

"*Marco*," Contessa called, as if they were playing a devilish game of hide and seek.

Modem rested her hand on his. "Is what you guys said true, about me never getting any older? Am I really gonna be like this forever?"

Jayden searched her eyes. "You weren't asleep, were you?"

She shook her head.

Modem had gone long enough being scared, lonely, and unsure. Even if it scared her, she deserved to know the truth.

He nodded. "Yeah." He forced a smile. "It's true. You'll never get old. Pretty cool, huh?"

Without a word, Modem simply turned her gaze forward. Staring into the barren distance, a low sob bubbled from her throat.

CHAPTER SIXTEEN

"I know it's all a lot to take in, but you can't have a breakdown. Not now." He squeezed Modem's small hand, grabbing her attention. "We need to find a way out of here."

"*Marco*," Contessa called a second time. Another root from the tree punched through Modem's barrier, shaking the wavering wall. "What a pity," Contessa said in a pouty tone. "A game is not sincerely a game unless there is a second party to play."

Modem's arm trembled. "I can't keep the wall up," she said in a whispered breath.

"Yes, you can. You can." She had to, or they wouldn't survive.

The ground at Jayden's feet pushed up, as if something were clawing to the surface. Jayden pulled back his feet and scrambled away, staring at the cracked dirt as it broke open, and a tiny root pushed through. "Oh no."

Now it was clear what she'd used the book for, and that they were too late.

There were no more hands. She'd used the book to drive underworld souls into her grasp. The souls that had clawed their way up from deeper realms of the underworld had made their way straight into her trap, and been consumed by her dark craving. And now the roots of the sacred tree were everywhere.

She had them right where she wanted them—trapped—just like the souls she had consumed.

"Hey." Modem smiled through shimmering tears that gleamed against the curves of her jaw. Her honey brown eyes held her familiar light. "Don't be scared."

Jayden stilled. "I'm supposed to be telling you that."

"Take care of Brisa, okay? She needs you."

Jayden narrowed his eyes. "Modem, what are you doing?"

"I can't do…this." She stared down at her hands splayed out in front of her. "Not forever."

"You'll be fine. We'll take care of you."

She shook her head. "No, you won't." She looked up at him. "You say that now, but even my own parents couldn't take care of me. No foster family will want me. I'll never find a place I belong."

Jayden rested his hand on her shoulder. "You belong with us."

"Maybe." She pushed to her feet, still shielded by the abandoned ancient ruin. More roots pushed up from the ground around them, slithering over the cracked, dry ground. "But Brisa belongs with you, and you need to get back to her. Plus," she shrugged, "I watched *Interview With a Vampire.*

Living forever is way overrated when you're stuck as a kid."

"Modem." His tone was more commanding. "We will find a way out of here. Just give me a minute—" He sucked in a breath and cringed away from a root crawling over his shoe. "We need to climb the ruin." He pulled himself up onto the first step.

Modem bit her bottom lip. "Okay. Let me just try to reinforce my barrier."

As Jayden climbed up to the second step, he stretched out his hand. "Come on. We don't have time." Dozens of roots pushed through the ground, growing faster and stronger as the tree punched more holes through the wavering barrier.

"I'll be right there." Modem drew an X over her chest and held up two fingers. "Promise."

Jayden's eyes widened and he tried to grab her arm, but she ran off before he could react. "Modem, no!" She darted around the side of the ancient ruin and out of sight. "Damn it, Modem!" He scrambled down, searching for a patch of soil to rest his foot, but the roots had taken over the ground, twisting and coiling around each other like an endless sea of venomous snakes. "Modem!" He scaled the height of the ruin, and then climbed as fast as he could up the narrow steps. He clung to the altar at the top, staring helplessly at the kid, who walked toward Contessa with a calm, poised posture.

He couldn't hear what they were saying, though he strained to communicate with Modem using his mind, like had in the middleworld. All he got was radio silence. She'd cut him off.

The watery wall wavered as more of Contessa's

black magic spread through it. Modem swayed on her feet, and a moment later, the barrier parted, creating an unprotected opening to the dark realm.

Jayden reached out. "Modem, run!"

Contessa's gaze snapped to where he stood. Her heinous grin taunted him.

A soft breath escaped his lungs. "No."

Contessa threw her hand forward, directing a root from the tree to lunge forward and punch through Modem's chest, throwing her to the ground.

"No!" Jayden leaped down the temple's stairs three at a time, flailing his arms to keep balance as shards of stone broke off under his feet. When he reached the ground, he stopped, his shoe teetering above the hungry roots.

Jayden locked eyes with Contessa as the tree fed on Modem, pulling her tiny body into the second layer of the underworld.

The rumble of rushing water sounded in the distance, but Jayden never looked away from the witch. His lip curled, and he balled his hands into fists as the wall of roaring water grew closer.

Contessa turned to face him, her chin lifted and her gaze full of contempt.

Jayden lifted his hand and pointed directly at her. "You can bet your ass I'm coming back for you."

The icy water plowed into him, making him gasp and claw his way to the surface.

When he woke, he opened his eyes to the smooth ceilings and crystal chandelier in the Marriott suite. Jay gasped and jumped to his feet.

Peter was hovering over Modem's body on the bed, pumping her chest with the palms of his hands and forcing several breaths into her lungs. "She's not responding!" He pumped her chest a few more times, paused, and then checked for a pulse. "Nothing. I'm losing her."

Hawa took Modem's hand and rubbed it, talking to her in a soft, sweet tone. Peter spread his hands over Modem's chest and closed his eyes, conjuring another round of his healing ability to bring her back.

"Come on, Modem. Come back to me." His fingers strained, pressing against her tiny body. Peter's normally pale face flushed with color, his eyebrows drawn together as his concentration deepened.

The room fell silent, and Peter opened his eyes. He stepped away from the kid, lying on the bed with one arm rested over her chest, the other limply hanging over the edge of the bed.

Peter shook his head. "I can't do anything else. She's gone."

"What do you mean she's gone?" Hawa braced her hands on both of Modem's shoulders and gently shook the girl against the mattress. "Hey." Hawa stilled, then shook her again. "Modem, you can get through this. You're tougher than this."

"Hawa." Jayden stepped forward, his throat tightening. "There's nothing you can do."

"No. You don't know Modem like I do." She brushed strands of kinky hair away from the girl's face.

"Maybe not, but some things you can't change."

Hawa turned her head and peered at him. "But you could have." She stood and squared her boots with her shoulders. "You were supposed to be watching her. You were supposed to protect her!" Hawa shoved Jayden in the chest, and then shoved him again, slamming his back into the dresser.

"You don't think I know that?" His pushed off the furniture. His nostrils flared. "I tried. We had nowhere to go. I told her not to—" His throat closed and he choked on the words.

"Whatever you have to say doesn't matter. You *failed*, and now she's *dead*." Hawa curled her lip and threw a punch at his jaw, but Jay blocked it with quick sideswipe, and then stepped aside.

"Hey!" Peter shouted. "Knock it—"

Hawa swung again, sloppier than before, and missed him entirely. Jayden shifted his weight, holding her gaze. "You don't have to do this. You've spent long enough torturing yourself over things you couldn't change." He glanced at her belly. "It's time to let go."

Hawa swayed, dragged her gaze to the girl, and fell to her knees. "I couldn't protect her." She sobbed into her hands, muffling her voice. It wasn't clear if she was talking about the baby or Modem— or maybe both. Either way, it didn't matter. Not anymore.

Jay knelt in front of her and pulled her against his chest. She melted into his embrace and coiled her arms around his neck. "I couldn't protect her," she whispered a second time.

He hugged her tight, running his hand down the length of her hair. There was nothing he could say to make it hurt any less, so he did what Zanya had told him he'd never done right in the past. He stayed quiet.

A few low sobs bubbled from her chest before she spoke again. "I want to go home."

***

Instead of taking a commercial plane, they boarded a private jet Renato had hired for the job. With Modem's coffin stored underneath, the luxury plane with leather seats and a private bar flew them home.

The commute was long, and nobody said much the entire way except for a few shortly worded whispers about getting a drink of water. Jayden peered out the window as they finally touched down on the runway of the private airport right outside of Toledo. Renato's SUV was parked near the gate, where a few workers in hardhats and neon vests stood, waiting for the jet to come to a complete stop.

Hawa laced his fingers between his. "Are you ready for this?"

He brushed his fingers over the top of her hand. "Which part?" There were so many uncertainties ahead, he couldn't pick just one.

"Everything." She rested her head on his shoulder and let out a soft exhale. "Being in the house without Zanya and Arwan. Not knowing if we even have a dog in the fight anymore. It's all so unsure."

Jay nodded. "It seems like there's nothing we can be sure about anymore."

She lifted her head and watched him. "I'm sure

140

about more than one thing." She squeezed his hand tighter. "I'm sure you tried your best to save her. I'm sorry I said any different."

A soft smile teased his lips.

"And I'm sure about you. Us."

It had only been a few days since Arwan and Zanya bonded, and any hope of winning her back was lost. It was like a raw kick in the balls when it happened—made his vision blur and stomach lurch into his throat.

But since he'd faced that reality, the cloud of fear he lived in had lifted, giving him a new take on the world around him—and the people. She'd been so close this entire time, but he never really saw her. Until now.

He leaned into her and pressed a kiss on her forehead. "I'm sure about that too."

The aircraft finally parked. Peter's seatbelt clanked when he unbuckled, and he grabbed his backpack from the overhead storage. "Come on." Peter looked at them both. "Let's get the hell off this plane."

Jayden couldn't have said it any better himself.

When the door opened, a narrow flight of stairs was rolled in place. The three of them scaled down to the black asphalt, Jay squinting against the bright sunlight.

The doors to Renato's SUV opened, and all three of them stepped out—Renato, Eleuia, and Marzena. They watched with sad eyes as the three teens walked toward them. Renato's warm gaze was more like Hawa's than he'd ever realized, and the sight of their mentor's fitted suit and combed, black hair was surprisingly comforting.

Hawa let go of Jay's hand and ran toward Renato. She wrapped her arms around him and buried her face in his chest. Renato hugged her, resting his chin on the top of her head, but his eyes stayed focused on Jayden.

When Jay and Peter approached the SUV, Marzena stepped aside. She bowed her head, allowing long waves of golden hair to fall on either side of her face, as if granting a moment of silence for their loss.

Jayden paused beside her and examined the childlike features of the dreamwalker. "I'm sorry," he said in a low voice, prompting Marzena to lift her gaze. Her bright green eyes were wide and searching. "I know Modem was one of yours." Jayden looked away. "She was one of us."

"For someone who's already dead, I can't believe you're alive." Zanya's mother walked around the front of the car. "It's good to see you all home."

Peter stepped forward. "Thanks. It's good to be back."

Hawa finally let go of her uncle and took her place beside Jayden. "What are we going to do with Mode—" She cleared her throat. "With Chastity?"

Renato gestured to the airport workers unloading a tiny white coffin from the cargo area of the plane. "We're going to give her the honor she deserves."

Jayden nodded. "And then?"

Renato stood up straighter, one hand curled around the lapel of his dark dress coat. "We seek our revenge."

BIRTHRIGHT

Book 5 of
The Stone Legacy Series

The thrilling conclusion to:
The Stone Legacy Series

Chapter One

Zanya

The road was deserted just outside the city of Tikal. The car was quiet, and the air was thick with tension, making it harder and harder to breathe.

Zanya slouched in the passenger seat and pulled her knees to her chest. "I can't believe that just happened." She combed her fingers through her hair, pulling brown, wavy strands away from her flushed cheeks. "I don't understand. I mean…" Her bottom lip trembled through her effort to hide it. "My mom wanted me to choose between you and her. How could she?"

Arwan trained his gaze on the long, straight highway, gripping the steering wheel until his knuckles turned dusky, and the tendons that wound up his forearm bulged with every movement. "She should understand." He flexed his jaw. "She fell in love with a human once, even though nobody approved of their love."

"But they never bonded," Zanya said. Humans

and Riyata couldn't bond, but then again… She dragged her focus to Arwan's angled jaw and dark, piercing eyes. "We shouldn't have been able to bond. What happened back there?"

For the first time, he tore his attention away from the road and examined her. "I don't know."

The lights of aurora never should have chosen her and Arwan to be soul mates. He as part underworlder, and she as the Stone Guardian. They were incompatible, or so they were told.

A flutter rolled over Zanya's belly as she looked into Arwan's smoky eyes. It was just hours ago, while standing on the grassy hill that overlooked the solstice celebration, she was sure any hope of them being together was lost forever. Now her world had been turned upside-down, and their bond had been sealed. The heaven spirits, the gods of Tamoanchan, must have seen something in him. Something that made him worthy.

"Where are we going?" she said in a low tone.

"Into the city. We'll at least have a place to spend the night."

Heat wound around her muscles and crawled down the backs of her legs. Spend the night? Together? After their bonding, it never occurred to her what came next. She flushed just from being near him, let alone staying the night with him.

Besides, her first solstice was over and the effect it had on her carnal instincts was supposed to have worn off. Apparently, that wasn't the case. It didn't help she sensed the anchor of their bond deep in her bones. Her cheeks flushed with another rush of heat.

Arwan turned his attention back to the road. "Are

you okay?"

Zanya tucked hair behind her ear. "Yeah, I think so. Why?"

"I can hear your heart racing."

She let out a long exhale. "Right. I forgot about that whole instinct thing."

He grinned, ever so slightly. "At least you're not crying anymore."

Her soft smile vanished from her lips as her mind flashed back to her mother's death glare and rigid shoulders. She really hated Arwan, with every fiber of her being. The way she glared at them standing together was chilling. Her mother had never seemed so cold.

"We'll stop at an ATM, and then find a hotel. I'll call Renato. He'll know what we should do."

"An ATM? Did Renato give you a bank card or something?"

"No." He stole another glance at her. "I have some savings stored away."

"Savings?" As far as she knew, he'd spent his entire life at Renato's house. "How did you save anything? I thought you'd never lived outside of Toledo."

His features grew sober. "I inherited enough to keep us comfortable."

"Inherited?" From his mother who abandoned him? That didn't sound like something a careless woman would do. But it was too sore of a topic to bring up now, and in all honesty, it wasn't important. As long as they had enough money to eat and keep a roof over their heads until they figured out what to do, everything would be okay.

As long as she was with him, it didn't matter.

Zanya rested her head on the side of the car they'd taken from the solstice celebration—another issue they'd have to deal with later. The hum of the engine and the muffled roar of wind flowing through the cracked windows relaxed her rigid muscles. She reached up and skimmed her fingers over the wicker pendant Cualli had given her.

Her stone vibrated from the pouch it was tucked away in, on the bracelet her mother had given her. She sucked in a tiny breath. Her stone. It must have been terrified after everything that'd happened, even though it had never translated that to her.

She opened the pouch and slipped her stone into the palm of her hand. "Hey." She held it between her fingers and rolled it around. "Sorry. I know it's a lot to take in." The stone illuminated with hues of blue and white, rolling with magic. Streaks of joy and comfort rushed through her—translated from her stone. "Hm. Not so tough then, huh?" She smiled and glanced at Arwan. "Yeah, he's not so bad."

"I suppose I'll have to get used to you talking to your rock?" He snickered.

"Shh." She hugged it against her chest. "It'll hear you call it a rock."

"And?" Arwan's eyes lit up. "What's it going to do?"

"You shouldn't be afraid of what *it'll* do." She pressed her index finger on his biceps and summoned a pulse of electrify to course over her hand. The shock sparked when it kissed his skin.

He swerved and shouted. "Are you trying to kill

us both?" He rubbed his arm, still half-grinning.

Zanya couldn't tear her gaze away from his caramel skin and dark lashes. Away from his lips.

His grin spread. "Your heart is racing again."

She blew out a puff of air and slouched back in her seat. "You've got to stop using your heightened senses for your personal advantage."

He rested his hand on her thigh. "Why?"

She suppressed the urge to gasp as heat spread over her skin where he touched.

She hadn't been with anyone before. Jayden was her first real boyfriend—if there was such a thing in a mental institution—but they'd never gotten past second base. It was all too much to wrap her mind around at once.

Arwan slid his hand down to her knee and squeezed it, just once, before returning his hand to the wheel, as if he knew what she was thinking.

The heat gripping her lungs gradually cooled, but not before she realized the light in her chest had flickered on. A dead giveaway.

She drew in a slow, deep breath and turned on the radio. Some music would help pass the time, at least until they got to the city. Then they'd call Renato and find out when it was safe to go home.

Something told her it would be a while, if ever, before her mother would welcome them back.

***

Arwan had driven through the night, watching the secluded desert terrain morph into wide highways and twinkling lights from towering buildings. Zanya had been asleep for almost an hour. Her rhythmic breathing and steady heartbeat kept him calm as he searched for an explanation. She was right. They never should have been allowed to bond.

He grabbed his cellphone from the cup holder and swiped his finger across the screen. He'd hoped to talk to Renato in private. This would have to do. Once Zanya woke, he didn't want to shut her out, though he didn't want to alarm her with his conversation to Renato, in case anything unexpected came up.

He tapped his thumb on the screen and pressed the phone to his ear. It rang just once before Renato picked up.

"Arwan. Are you two all right?"

"Yeah. We're okay."

"Where are you?"

"Driving." After a few nights in a random hotel, he still didn't know where they'd go. "We're both confused, and Zanya is still trying to wrap her mind around her mother's ultimatum."

"I know. I'm sure you are both very shaken up. Ellie hasn't given Marzena a moment's rest since you two left, begging her to somehow connect with Zanya using her ability. She's terribly worried for Zanya's safety. She still believes you're going to hurt her."

Arwan tensed. The mention of anyone hurting Zanya drove a spike of fear up his spine, followed by a rush of searing heat that simmered in his gut. He'd protect her from anyone or anything, no matter what, and with his life. "Tell Marzena we appreciate her giving us our privacy."

"Of course. I've spent every waking moment researching, trying to understand exactly what happened. The gods of Tamoanchan must have somehow blessed your union with—" There was a brief pause. "Your bond. How could I have neglected to congratulate you? I'm terribly sorry. It's just that under the circumstances—"

"Don't worry about that, Renato." The corners of his mouth curled as he admired Zanya for a moment, curled into a ball, still deeply asleep. "Thank you. It's…" His chest tightened as the link between them deepened, boring into his soul. "It's nothing like I ever thought possible. I don't…" To say it aloud felt somehow wrong, but it was the absolute truth. "I don't hate myself anymore. It's like I'm finally at peace."

"That's truly outstanding. I couldn't be happier for you both, even if the union is somewhat unconventional. How is Zanya coping with the bond? Neither of you expected it, and I'm sure the sudden link has had a jarring impact on you both."

"So far we're both handing the bond fairly well." In fact, not a lot had changed for him. He had always been connected to Zanya. Even before Drina interpreted the passage from the book of Popul Vuh, revealing they were truly destined for each other, he somehow knew.

"Very good. Please keep a close watch over her, as I know you will. I'll work to get Ellie under control and find a way to bring both of you back."

Arwan nodded. "Okay. Meanwhile, Zanya and I are going to stay in the city."

"Why would you choose to stay there?"

Arwan furrowed his brow. "What choice do we have?"

Renato was silent for a long moment. "There is a second option. Perhaps it's time you went home."

Arwan's throat tightened as he pulled the car to a stop on the emergency shoulder. "Home?" He gripped the wheel tighter with one hand. "What are you talking about?"

Renato breathed into the phone—the kind of breath you let out when you dreaded what you were about to say. "Do you remember the home you grew up in, before you came to Toledo? Before you lived with me?"

Arwan slowly shook his head. He could barely remember what his mother looked like, let alone his childhood home. If it weren't for the sketches hung on his bedroom wall in Renato's house, and the brief moment he got to watch her through Contessa's magical haze in Moscow, he probably would have forgotten her entirely.

"I'll take your silence as a no," Renato said. "Spend as long as you'd like in the city, but when you're ready, travel to Mexico."

"Mexico?" His breaths became quicker. "Is that where I'm from?"

"That is where you were born, and where you spent your childhood."

Arwan clutched his chest as his darker half clawed at him. He was usually able to ignore it, but with his recent bonding, perhaps that was the one difference he'd have to watch out for. "The house is still there? You're sure?" It had been nearly fifte years since he'd left his home, when he was just six years old.

"I received a piece of mail many years ago with nothing but the deed to the home in your mother's name, postmarked. I could only assume it was your mother who sent it, as it wasn't signed, and there was no note to accompany it.

"Why didn't you tell me this before? You gave me my inheritance, but not this? I should have known—" He clamped his teeth and clutched his chest tighter. His darker half whipped and burrowed into him. Arwan groaned and leaned into the steering wheel.

"Are you all right, Arwan?" Renato's voice was muffled in his ears. He drew in a shaky breath, concentrating on putting his darker half at rest. Soon, it settled down and became dormant again.

"Send me the address," he said softly, not wanting to wake Zanya and worry her. "I have to go."

Arwan hung up the phone and tossed it in the back seat, then mounted both hands on the wheel and stared ahead. His palms were clammy and his head throbbed from the rush of darkness slithering through him.

He'd have to push past it and keep driving, all the way to the airport.

ABOUT THE AUTHOR

A long time enthusiast of things that go bump in the night, Theresa began her writing career as a journalism intern—possibly the least creative writing field out there. After her first semester at a local newspaper, she washed her hands of press releases and features articles to delve into the whimsical world of young adult paranormal romance.

Since then, Theresa has gotten married, had three terrific kids, moved to central Ohio, and was repeatedly guilt tripped into adopting a menagerie of animals that are now members of the family. But don't be fooled by her domesticated appearance. Her greatest love is travel. Having stepped foot on the soil of over a dozen countries, traveled to sixteen U.S. states—including an extended seven-year stay in Kodiak, Alaska—she is anything but settled down.

Wherever life brings her, she will continue to weave tales of adventure and love with the hope her stories will bring joy and inspiration to her readers.

Author's Note:

Thank you for reading Anarchy. Want an advance notice of the next release and exclusive content? Sign up for Theresa's mailing list.

Reviews mean so much and help others find books. If you enjoyed Anarchy, please leave a review, even if it's a short one.